"We're engaged?" Alejandro sent Catriona a look.

With the bright lights gleaming from the house, this one was easy to interpret. He was *amused*?

"It's your fault," she declared, instantly defensive. "I was trying not to be predictable. You dared me."

"So it's *my* fault?"

"This entire mess is your fault." She nodded firmly.

He slowly stepped closer. "You don't feel any responsibility, given you're the one who broke in and tried to steal from me?"

"I didn't break in—I used a key. And I wasn't stealing anything that belongs to you."

"No? I wonder." He was watching her closely, then his smile returned, slow and seductive. "Catriona, you are going to pay for this, you know."

"Not in the way you're thinking."

He laughed and stepped closer so he was right in her personal space. "Very much in the way I'm thinking. You think these sparks can be ignored?"

Natalie Anderson adores a happy ending—which is why she always reads the back of a book first. Just to be sure. So you can be sure you've got a happy ending in your hands right now—because she promises nothing less. Along with happy endings she loves peppermint-filled dark chocolate, pineapple juice and extremely long showers. Not to mention spending hours teasing her imaginary friends with dating dilemmas. She tends to torment them before eventually relenting and offering—you guessed it—a happy ending. She lives in Christchurch, New Zealand, with her gorgeous husband and four fabulous children.

If, like her, you love a happy ending, be sure to come and say hi on Facebook.com/authornataliea, follow @authornataliea on Twitter, or visit her website/blog: natalie-anderson.com.

Books by Natalie Anderson

Harlequin Presents

The Forgotten Gallo Bride
Pleasured by the Secret Billionaire
Mistress Under Contract
Bought: One Night, One Marriage
His Mistress by Arrangement

The Throne of San Felipe

The Secret that Shocked De Santis
The Mistress that Tamed De Santis

The Royal House of Karedes

Ruthless Boss, Royal Mistress

Harlequin Kiss

Whose Bed Is It Anyway?
The Right Mr. Wrong

Visit the Author Profile page at Harlequin.com for more titles.

Natalie Anderson

—

CLAIMING HIS
CONVENIENT FIANCÉE

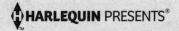

Recycling programs
for this product may
not exist in your area.

ISBN: 978-0-373-06084-9

Claiming His Convenient Fiancée

First North American Publication 2017

Copyright © 2017 by Natalie Anderson

Printed in U.S.A.

CLAIMING HIS
CONVENIENT FIANCÉE

This one is for the nurses—Olivia, Akansha, Gavin, Glenda, Jo (and Arnie!), Karl, Maria, Naomi, Salma, Shannon and Shannon and all the others who have helped us...you guys are amazing. Thank you so much for everything, not least teaching us Beanie!

CHAPTER ONE

FRENETIC DRUM AND bass reverberated down the dark street. Irritation pulsed along Kitty Parkes-Wilson's veins, keeping time with the relentless beat. It was too much to hope the neighbours would complain; no doubt they were wishing they could be at the party, all desperate to suck up to the rich new blood on the block.

Alejandro Martinez. Former management consultant turned venture capitalist. Millionaire. Promiscuous playboy. Party animal. And, since signing the documents three days ago, proud owner of the beautiful building in the heart of London that had, until said three days ago, been her family home. The home she'd grown up in, the one that had been in the family for more than five generations until her father had seized the wad of cash Alejandro Martinez had waved under his nose and skipped off to his sunny retirement villa in Corsica with his third picture-book-pretty wife. He'd cleared his debts and abandoned his failed business—and floored children.

All of which Kitty could handle. Just. Anyway, as much as she'd have liked to, the fact was she couldn't have bought Parkes House herself. But she hadn't even been told before it had been sold, and something had inadvertently been left in the Edwardian mansion. Something her father didn't own and had no right to sell. And *that* she couldn't cope with. Kitty Parkes-Wilson was on a retrieval mission and nothing and no one was going to stop her.

It wasn't the necklace's material worth that made it so important. Its loss meant her twin, Teddy, was in trouble, and her own *heart* was in trouble.

'You *can't* do this.'

She grinned at the way her brother could sound both aghast and excited.

'You can't stop me—I'm already here,' she answered in a low voice, pressing her phone closer to her ear as she slowed down her pace just before arriving at her former home. 'And you know I can do it.'

'Damn it, Kitty, you're crazy,' Teddy growled. 'You're only just off the train; why do you have to rush into this? Come here and we can talk about it.'

If she stopped to talk about it too much, she'd lose her nerve. 'The sooner I get it back the better. Now's the perfect chance, what with the party and all.'

'But what if you get caught—?'

'I won't,' she impatiently interrupted. 'He'll be too busy partying with his models to notice me.'

Alejandro Martinez only dated supermodels, trading them in with efficient regularity. According to the theatre gossip Teddy had shared when he'd told her that the house was being sold, the current model was Saskia, the number one swimwear model in the North American sports magazine market. Kitty figured that with those legs to distract him, Mr Martinez would never notice the quick in-and-out of an uninvited party guest. Especially one who knew the secrets of the house and how to stay hidden as she snuck her way to the second-floor library.

'It's in the library post, right?' She ignored her stomach's hungry rumble and double-checked with her twin. 'You're sure about that?'

'Positive.' Her brother's tone changed to out-and-out concerned again. 'But Kitty, please, I'm really not sure—'

'I'll call you as soon as I'm clear, okay? Stop worrying.' She ended the call before he could reply.

Adrenalin amped her muscles. She needed to concentrate and keep her confidence high. With a quick glance each way along the street, she quietly braced then hopped the fence. She ditched her small carry-on bag between a couple of shrubs and got to work.

Alejandro Martinez was not getting his hands on her Great-Aunt Margot's diamond choker. He was not putting it on any of his many girlfriends. Kitty would go to prison before she let that happen. It was not a flashy bauble for a temporary lover.

The back door key was still hidden in the same spot of the communal gated garden where she'd first hidden it a decade before. No one but she and Teddy knew it existed or that it was there and so, despite the sale of the property, it hadn't been handed to the new owner. She recovered it in less than ten seconds.

Phase one: complete.

She turned to look at the house. Brightly lit and in beautiful condition on the outside at least, it appeared to be the gleaming jewel in a row of similar styles. But Kitty knew the truth hidden beneath that freshly painted facade.

She made short work of the fence again then
crossed to the corner of the street and found her way
to the mews laneway behind the mansions. Her heart
hammered as she neared the rear of the house. The
lights were on, and she could see a catering worker
at the sink.

That was when she threw her shoulders back and
lifted her chin.

She unlocked the door, stepped in and smiled
blithely at the kitchen hand, who looked up and gazed
at her in astonishment. She waved the key at him and
held her finger to her perfectly reddened lips. 'Don't
tell him I'm here—I want to surprise him,' she said
as she confidently strolled past him and out into the
corridor.

The dishwashing chap didn't stop her. He didn't
say anything. He just turned back to the plate he was
rinsing.

She'd learned a few things from sitting in on Teddy's drama classes over the years.

*Act confident. Fake it till you make it. Act like you
own the place and people will believe you do.*

People chose to believe the easiest option—the least
trouble for them. And with her walking in all smiles,
and with a key, who would doubt her right to be there?

Phase two: complete.

All she had to do now was head up the stairs to
the private library, retrieve the necklace and get out
again as fast as possible.

But curiosity bit. It had been months since she'd
been home and now her heart ached with nostalgia
for what she'd lost. In the three days since he'd taken
over, what changes had Alejandro Martinez made?

Apparently he'd liked the look of the street and knocked on everyone's doors to find someone willing to sell. Her father hadn't been willing—he'd been *desperate*. Alejandro had been the answer to all his prayers. And Alejandro had got a good deal. House. Contents. Even the cars.

Winding up the company was one thing, but for her father to sell this home without saying a word to them beforehand was unforgivable. He'd sold everything *in* the house as well—only stopping to parcel up the few personal papers left in here. There were things she and Teddy might have liked, family treasures that had sentimental value. She didn't care about the monetary side of things; she'd grown up knowing most of it would never be hers. Her father hadn't thought of her—then again, he never had. But for once he'd not thought about Teddy either. Not that Teddy cared—he was glad not to have any reminders of the expectation he could never live up to. Except there was the last legacy from Great-Aunt Margot— the one Kitty had got her hair colour from, the one who'd given Kitty what confidence and fun she had. Great-Aunt Margot was her inspiration.

Kitty ventured down the corridor towards the bubble of music and chatter and laughter and glanced through the open doorway into the atrium.

The lighting there was much dimmer than in the kitchen. The guests probably thought it was low to set the 'mood' and make everyone look even more attractive, but they really didn't need the help. No, the soft lighting was all about helping hide the aged, peeling paintwork and how much refurbishment and restoration work the house needed. It seemed Alejandro had had no hesitation in stripping the house of all its 'maximalist' decor—all the antique furniture, vases and fine china displays had vanished, and in their place were three dozen nubile, beautiful women. Every last one had to be a model. Kitty's heart puckered. It was weird to have all these other women here, all relaxed and happy and looking as if they belonged, when she no longer did.

Stopping to look had been a mistake.

She skirted the back of the room to confidently—but not too quickly—walk up the stairs. She kept her head high, her shoulders back and sent a glimmer of a smile to the person she saw along the hallway glancing up after her.

Faking it. Making it.

The volume of the music lowered the higher up the stairs she went. By the time she got to the second floor it had become bearable background noise. There was no one in sight up here—the entire house had yet to be taken over by pumped-up party people. She'd timed her arrival just right—enough people were present for her to disappear into, but it wasn't yet wild enough for them to be everywhere.

Despite the disappointment of seeing the stripped out interior below, she couldn't resist pausing by the master bedroom. The door was open—inviting her—but when she peered carefully around it, she found she couldn't step into the room. It was stuffed with boxes and furniture. So this was where everything from downstairs had been shoved. Her heart ached more and she quickly stepped along the hallway. Unfortunately, the library door was closed. She hovered a moment to listen, but heard nothing coming from within the room. Nervously, she turned the handle. To her relief it was dark inside and apparently unoccupied. She knew that if she left the door open, enough light would spill from the corridor for her to find her way. She smiled in anticipation as she lightly tiptoed to the shelves lining the farthest wall. This house had several secrets that the new owner would never know about—her father wouldn't have thought to tell him any of it. Sure, the pleasure she felt at having knowledge over Alejandro Martinez was childish, but the way he'd waltzed in and snatched away her home made her smart.

On the fifth shelf up, behind the fourth book along from the left, there was a small lever. She depressed it and listened to the scratchy whirring sound as a small cavity opened up. She didn't need to take the other books out; it was only a tiny safe—only large enough for a pile of notes written by bored children, or a coil of diamonds in a platinum setting left there by her forgetful, beloved, fool of a brother.

Kitty scooped them up, relief washing through her. She'd half expected them not to be there—Teddy's recollections weren't always accurate. But they were *hers* again and she could get them back to where they belonged. She'd hated the thought of letting Margot down—even though Margot was only alive in memory now.

Swallowing hard, she straightened the chain and put it around her neck, angling her head as she secured the clasp and then ran her finger along her throat to ensure the choker was sitting smoothly. The cold heaviness was familiar and made her heart ache all over again.

These were the only diamonds Margot had ever worn. She'd bought them for herself, by herself. She'd declared that she needed no man to buy her jewels and had lived her life in defiant independence, refusing to settle into any kind of expectation—ahead of her time and leaving Kitty in awe.

She wished the choker could be hers for good, but it was Teddy's birthright and he'd given up everything else already. Kitty had nothing to lose.

She released her hair from the high topknot she'd coiled it into while on the train. To leave looking different from how she'd arrived was part of the plan and her hair served another purpose now—it mostly hid the gleaming necklace. She pushed the lever again and the compartment slid shut.

Phase three: complete.

Satisfied, she turned, ready to leave.

That was when she saw it—the man's silhouette looming in the doorway. She froze. With the lack of light she couldn't see his face, but she could see he held a phone in his hand. And she could see how tall he was. How broad. How impossible to slip past.

'Hello?' She wished she didn't sound so scared.

She wished he'd answer.

Her heart took two seconds to start pumping again and when it did her pulse thumped loudly in her ears. She hadn't heard him arrive. The floor in the library was wooden and she'd been certain she'd have heard approaching footsteps. But apparently this guy could enable stealth mode. Was he Security? How long had he been watching her? Had he seen what she'd done?

Apprehension fluttered in her belly.

'She wasn't wearing a necklace when she arrived,'

he slowly mused. Softly. Dangerously. 'Yet she wears one now.'

She froze at that accented English, at that tone. She was definitely in trouble.

'If you'd get your boss for me, I can explain,' she bluffed haughtily.

'My name is Alejandro Martinez,' he replied, still in those soft, dangerous tones that made her skin prickle. 'I am the boss.'

It was the devil himself. Of course. Kitty's heart thundered.

He reached out a hand, casually closing the door. There was a split second of total darkness before he unerringly turned on the light.

Kitty rapidly blinked at the brightness. By the time the dancing spots cleared from her vision, he was less than a foot from her, his phone gone and his hands free.

She swallowed.

He was very close and *very* tall. She wasn't short yet she had to tip her chin to look into his face. His hair was dark brown and thick and he was so good-looking, he ought to have been outlawed as hazardous to any woman's attention span. Yes, Alejandro Martinez was fiendishly handsome with that olive skin, those chiselled features and those serious, assessing eyes.

Nervously, she flicked her hair in the hopes it would curl around her throat. She wasn't getting past him in a hurry; there was only one exit out of this library and he'd closed the door.

'No, there's no point trying to hide it now,' he mocked softly, but his eyes glittered like polished onyx. He slowly lifted a lock of her hair back with a lazy, arrogant finger. His penetrating gaze lingered on her neck, then raked down her body—her breasts, her waist, her legs. Every inch of her felt grazed.

'A diamond collar for a lithe little cat burglar,' he said. 'How appropriate.'

To her horror, her body reacted to his unabashed sensual assessment of her and to his low accented tone. Her skin tightened. Heat flooded her cheeks, her lower belly and she fought the instinct to take a squirming step back.

Alejandro Martinez was so *not* her cup of tea. Too obvious. Too forceful. Too…everything.

'A ginger she-cat,' he added thoughtfully, his focus lifting to her face. 'Rather rare.'

She bristled. She'd always hated her hair. She'd gone through a phase when she'd dyed it darker, only that had made her almost see-through skin and squillions of freckles look worse. In the end she'd given up and gone back to natural and faced the fact she was never going to be a 'beauty'.

'You know about the bookcase?' she asked, trying to take control of the situation—of herself—and draw attention away from this *awareness*. But her voice sounded husky and uncertain. She had to get herself and the necklace out of here as fast as possible.

'I do now. What other secrets do you know about this house?' His gaze seemed to penetrate right through her. 'What else are you planning to steal?'

A hot streak of stubbornness shot through her. She wasn't going to tell him anything—not about the house, not about herself, not about the necklace.

So she just stared up at him silently, waiting for him to make his next move.

His expression hardened. 'Give me the necklace,' he said firmly.

She shook her head. 'Possession is nine-tenths of the law,' she muttered.

'Possession?' He suddenly looked even more intent, even more predatory as his jaw sharpened and his eyes gleamed as they locked on hers.

Heat unfurled low in her belly. Shocking, utterly unwanted, destructive heat.

'It is very valuable,' he noted, continuing to watch her way too closely for her comfort. Standing too close too. When had he moved closer?

Kitty struggled to keep her brain working. The necklace was valuable, but not only in the way *he* meant. It was all heart and memory to her.

'You know it's not yours,' she said, determinedly meeting his gaze and refusing to step back and show his intimidation was working.

'I am also willing to bet it's not yours.' His return gaze was ruthless. His stance was implacable.

But all that did was fire Kitty's desire to defy him. This man had taken ownership of everything she loved. He wasn't having this too. But she couldn't halt the telltale guilty heat building in her cheeks.

The diamonds might not belong to her legally, but they were hers in her heart. Damn Teddy's uselessness. 'It's mine to retrieve.'

And hers by love. No one loved this necklace more than her—more than that, she'd loved the woman who'd once owned it.

Alejandro shook his head slowly. 'This building and everything in it belongs to me now.' A small smile hovered at his mouth. 'Seeing as you are so insistent to stay, I guess that includes you too.'

Oh, she did *not* belong to anyone—and most certainly not him. This display of ownership was outrageous and beyond arrogant. 'Actually, I was just leaving,' she snapped coldly.

'No.' That tantalising smile vanished and he firmly grasped her wrist.

Kitty couldn't hide the tremble that rippled through her as she fisted her hand and tried to pull free from him.

'I think that both the necklace and you will remain in my possession until we find the rightful owner.' His eyes glinted. 'Of both.'

Defiance burned, sharpening her senses. Surely he was just being provocative, except she had the feeling he meant it. He was clearly used to being in control and having all the power. She didn't want to tell him the truth about the diamonds. She wouldn't try to appeal to his sensitive side—it was all too obvious he didn't have one. Arrogant jerk.

The pressure on her wrist grew—inexorably he drew her closer.

'What are you doing?' she gasped when he firmly ran his other hand across her stomach.

Alejandro didn't answer as he swept his palm further around her waist. She was a slim thing and had little in the way of curves, most unlike the women he usually spent time with. And yet there was something undeniably attractive about her. Undeniably different. She was clad entirely in black—slim three-quarter-length trousers and a fitted black sweater that emphasised her tall but slender frame. Her eyes screamed outrage and he suppressed a smile at the stiffness of her body as he continued his search. Maybe that was it—she presented resistance, challenge. And for him that was novel.

'You're assaulting me?' she snarled venomously.

'Checking for a concealed weapon,' he answered smoothly, but a grim defensiveness rose within at her accusation. Alejandro Martinez would *never* assault any woman. He was not like—*no*.

He forced his attention to his pretty prisoner, not his past. Her eyes were the weapons here and now, striking like twin daggers and making him smile, a respite from the memory that had flickered. Pleased, he removed the phone from where she'd tucked it into the waistband of her trousers.

He released her to study his prize. The phone wasn't the latest model and had one of those covers that had a pocket for a couple of cards—a bank card and driver's licence tucked inside. Perfect.

'Catriona Parkes-Wilson.' He read the name aloud, glancing to watch her reaction to the identification.

Soft colour bloomed in her pale cheeks again, and her emerald eyes flashed. She really was striking.

'Kitty,' she corrected him quickly.

Catriona—Kitty—Parkes-Wilson was the daughter of the man who'd sold him this house.

Alejandro would have guessed that the diamonds—undoubtedly real—would be hers, but she'd looked so guilty when he'd stopped her that he now wondered. He had to be certain of their provenance before relinquishing them to her just like that.

But finally he understood her presence here tonight. She was on a retrieval mission.

She was also the ultimate in spoilt heiresses—so headstrong and so used to getting her way that she thought she could strut straight into any room and take what she wanted. Why not do the normal polite thing and *ask*? The sleek Catriona seemed only able to take. And no doubt she was used to causing trouble with every step.

He dampened down the rising attraction and told himself it would be fun to teach her a lesson in politeness, and *then* possession.

'Catriona…' he repeated her full name, deliberately ignoring her preference, and couldn't stop his smile when she looked more annoyed '…I'm delighted to have you back in your former residence. Welcome.'

His security detail had informed him of her unorthodox arrival via text but Alejandro had already spotted her from his hidden vantage point upstairs where he'd been having a moment away from his guests. She'd climbed the stairs as though she thought she was invisible. As if hair the sparkling colours of an autumnal bonfire could ever blend into the background. Even when it had been tied in that pile on her head it had caught his attention. Now that it hung loose in a tumble of crazy curls, he was tempted to tangle his fingers into it and draw her close for a kiss…

But he wasn't about to give in to this unexpected burst of desire.

Alejandro enjoyed sex and had no shortage of it, but it had been a while since he'd felt such an instant surge of lust for a woman. It was mildly irritating—he had better control than this and, to prove that to himself, he wasn't about to explore the sexual electricity arcing between them right now. Not yet. It would be more amusing to put this petulant princess in her place. He'd met too many spoilt people who'd never had to do a real day's work in their lives and who had no idea what hardship really was. Catriona Parkes-Wilson needed to learn some genuine manners.

An idea came instantly, as they generally did, but this one made his muscles tighten in a searing burst of anticipation.

'Remain here this evening as my date,' he said bluntly. 'Or I call the police. The choice is yours.'

'Your *date*?' Her eyes widened in surprise.

He knew she felt the sensual awareness the way he did. It seemed she didn't like it all that much either. Inexplicably, that improved his mood. He'd have her apology. And then, if it was good, maybe he'd have her.

'The police?' she suddenly added quickly, almost hopefully.

That threat was the lesser of the two evils to her? He needed to make that option more alarming. 'Your fingerprints are all over—'

'They would be anyway,' she interrupted scornfully. 'I lived here, remember?'

'And I have security camera footage.' He smiled. That silenced her.

'I can't ignore my guests for hours while I iron out this interruption of yours,' he said. 'So you will remain with me until I have the time to deal with you.'

Her eyes didn't waver from his as he stipulated his rules.

'I don't intend to leave your side even for a second,' he informed her quietly, failing to suppress the satisfaction that rose at the thought. 'Slinky cats can be clever escape artists. I'm not having you slip out when I look away for a second.' He read the fire in her gaze and his blood heated. 'And I do expect you to behave.'

Kitty glared at him. The thought of staying as his date should appal her. But what really shocked her was the delicious *anticipation* that shivered down her spine at the thought of such relentless attentiveness from him. What was *wrong* with her?

He bent closer, those full lips twisted ever so slightly into that tantalising smile. Dear Lord, he was too handsome.

'Catriona,' he said softly.

Now he loomed over her. She couldn't tear her gaze away from the bottomless depths of his black eyes. Her mouth parted as she struggled to breathe because her heart was thundering. Anticipation spiralled through every cell. Was he going to kiss her? Was she going to let him? Where had her *will* gone?

He was so close now she could feel his breath on her skin and his eyes were mesmerising and she simply couldn't seem to *move*. Then she felt the warmth of his fingers as he brushed the skin at the nape of her neck. She shivered, drawing in a shocked breath, but it was too late. He'd undone the clasp of the necklace before she'd registered his true intention. Now she could only stare as he stepped back and poured the glittering chain into his inside top pocket—right over the spot where his heart should be. Not that he had one of those.

He'd taken the diamond choker from her and she'd just let him.

She'd stood there like a vacant fool and let him reclaim the necklace. She'd let his good looks and his sexual magnetism render her *brainless*. How stupid could she get?

'I can't be your date,' she snapped, furious with herself.

'Why not?'

'You have a girlfriend already.'

'I do?' He sent her a penetrating look.

'Saskia something.' She straightened and snarled, venting her annoyance on him, 'I'm not helping you cheat on another woman.' She knew how much that sucked. 'Not even pretend cheating. So go ahead and call the police.'

She didn't think for a second he would but, to her apprehension, he pulled his mobile from his pocket again.

Had she misread him? Did he want the police here, interrupting his terribly exclusive party? She'd have to explain all and wear yet more mortification, but that was better than letting this man win. Surely the police would let her off with a warning—as a first time offender, distraught by the loss of her family home and all that... She might even be able to keep Teddy's name out of it.

She watched, breathing rapidly and still feeling too hot, as he held the phone up to his ear.

'Saskia, darling. I wanted to be honest with you and let you know before you heard it from anyone else.' He didn't hesitate. 'I've met someone else.'

Kitty's jaw dropped. He'd phoned the latest model girlfriend? She stared at him in frozen fascination as he kept talking.

'I know it seems sudden, but sometimes that's how life works.'

Had he just broken up with the woman?

OMG. The phone call was swift and to the point and the arrogant bastard smiled at *her* the entire way through.

'You just ended your relationship?' she all but gasped as he ended the call. 'Over the phone?'

'Four dates doesn't really constitute a relationship.' He shrugged and pocketed his mobile.

'And you never go much beyond five dates anyway.' Teddy had told her that. Apparently, Alejandro's appetite for a rapid succession of beauties caused frequent comment—celebration by some, such as Teddy, and derision from others. Kitty was firmly in the second camp.

His eyebrows flickered. 'Don't I? I don't tend to keep count.'

Of dates or women? 'You can't just do that.'

'I just did.'

'You don't care?' Was it all *that* meaningless for him? His callousness was repellent, yet there was still that fickle, stupid part of her that was attracted to him.

'No. I don't.' He laughed at her expression. 'She doesn't either. We both knew what we were in for.'

And what was that—a few meaningless hours in bed together? Kitty whipped up her anger on behalf of the woman. 'You're sure about that?'

'Utterly.' He looked bored as he glanced at his watch. 'Now you needn't have any scruples about being my date for the night.'

'No way.' She shook her head, still shocked at his

callous phone call. As if she'd ever date someone so ruthless. 'You're heartless.'

'If that's the case—' he reached for his pocket again '—then I will have to phone the police. Naturally, I will push for charges to be laid.' He sent her a mock-apologetic glance. 'It's unacceptable for people to unlawfully enter houses and take whatever they find lying around.'

She narrowed her eyes. He was playing a game. He'd have called the police already if that was what he'd really meant to do. 'You'll do whatever necessary to get what you want, won't you?'

He smiled as if that wasn't something to be ashamed of. 'Always.'

No doubt he'd blackmail, coerce, fight dirty and think nothing of it.

She gazed at him. He was hideously self-assured. Going through women like normal people went through pints of milk—on an almost daily basis and simply discarding the bottle when done. But that someone so shallow could be so attractive-looking? It was so wrong—the guy needed a warning label stamped on his forehead. Yet there was a whole roomful downstairs waiting to step up and be the next one. His looks and charisma had made things—women— far too easy for him.

He sent her that soft, suave smile, totally in control and at ease. 'What's it going to be, Catriona?' he prompted her gently. 'A night with me at your side, or a night in the cells?'

Her body recognised his beauty; her brain recognised he was a calculating bastard. She'd ensure her brain won this battle. She was certain he was not interested in her; he just wanted to teach her a lesson. That was obvious.

But *he* was the one who needed a lesson. The palm of her hand itched, but she'd never resorted to violence, not even in her worst attention-seeking teen tantrums and she wasn't letting this devil get to her in a way no one else ever had.

Nor was she letting him win. She had no idea what he thought he was going to achieve by forcing her to stay with him during his party, but she wasn't letting him have it. She'd make the night as difficult as possible for him. Then she'd tell the truth and demand Margot's diamonds back.

'Don't call the police,' she finally responded, answering demurely. 'I'll be your date.'

His eyes narrowed just the slightest, but his smile was ready and heart-stopping. He pocketed the phone again and then reached out and laced his fingers through hers. 'I never thought for a second that you wouldn't.'

CHAPTER TWO

'YOU'RE VERY SURE of yourself,' Kitty said, counting her breathing in an attempt to slow her speeding heart.

'I'm sure of people,' he answered. 'They are predictable.'

Well, he definitely wasn't predictable. And she *refused* to be—at least to him. 'What is it you want from me?' She tried to extricate her hand from his, but he wouldn't release her.

'What do you think I want from you?' That smile now lurked in his eyes.

Her chin lifted. 'If I knew, I wouldn't be asking.'

His glance sharpened, but he spoke calmly. 'Your time. Your undivided attention. And when every guest has gone tonight, we'll have a reckoning.'

Something flipped in her belly. Half horrified, half intrigued, she couldn't resist asking more. 'What kind of reckoning?'

The smile he flashed was nothing short of wicked. 'I think you've already guessed.'

He couldn't possibly mean *that*. She flushed. 'Never. Happening.'

He laughed then, releasing his grip on her to throw

both his hands in the air, surprisingly animated. 'See? Predictable.' That foreign element underlying his American accent had deepened deliciously.

He was teasing her? She shouldn't feel even a hint of disappointment. Yet she did. Alejandro Martinez was too much the practised flirt and too sure of his own attractiveness.

'I'm not in the least interested in you in that way,' she said, determined to make the point as clear as possible.

'Of course you're not,' he soothed, turning to lead the way to the door.

'I mean it. You try anything—'

He sighed theatrically. 'Well, it will be difficult, but I'll try to control my animal urges.'

Okay, so now she felt a fool because of course he wasn't really interested in her like that. He'd be back on the phone to his Saskia soon enough and sorting out the lovers' tiff or he'd be off with another of the models downstairs…

Laughter danced in his eyes as he turned and caught her glaring at his back.

'You are very beautiful when cross,' he said provocatively. 'Does that fiery hair bring a temper with it?'

She refused to answer him. Her hair didn't bring rage so much as rashness. Fool that she was, she should have listened to Teddy and calmed down before deciding to come on this crazy mission. She should at least have eaten something, then she wouldn't be feeling this light-headed.

He paused and waited until she'd looked up into

his face again before teasing her further. 'If you are a good date, you might get a reward.'

'All I want is the necklace,' she replied stiffly. And maybe some dinner at some point. Hopefully, there'd be some decent canapés downstairs and not just the tiny, calorie-free stuff that models lived on.

He took her hand firmly in his again and drew her towards the door. He was really serious about her mingling?

'What are you planning on telling your guests about me?' she asked.

A mystified expression crossed his face. 'Nothing.'

Clearly the opinion of others didn't bother him at all. Kitty tried very hard not to be bothered by what others thought, but there was still that soft part of her that ached to please someone. Anyone. Everyone.

She worked hard to fight it and protect her stupidly vulnerable heart. For too long her self-esteem had been bound up in the opinion of men. First her father. Then her fiancé.

She hesitated at the top of the stairs. Alejandro was already on the first step, but he turned. His eyes were almost at the same level as hers.

'Come on, my reluctant date,' he dared in that divine accent. 'Come down and act the mute martyr.'

Was *that* what he expected her to do?

She went from famished to galvanised in less than a second. She'd act the ultimate party person—something she hardly ever was. With just that one look from him her appetite vanished. It was her twin, Teddy, who usually held centre stage, while she was the quiet foil—always his most appreciative audience. But now? Now she was energised. Now she had a game to win.

'You're obviously very bored with your life.' She placed her hand on his upper arm, leaning close in a parody of an adoring, clinging lover—half hoping he'd pull away.

He didn't. His smile broadened. 'Because I have to coerce a beautiful woman into standing alongside me for the night?'

'Exactly. You must be very jaded,' she murmured, trying not to dwell on the size and hardness of the muscles she could feel under the fabric of his oh-so-perfectly tailored suit. 'Having to spice it up like this.'

He chuckled. 'I haven't the time to deal with you the way I want to right now; I need to spend time with my guests. We'll deal with each other properly later.'

She wasn't sure if that was a promise or a threat. Worse, she wasn't sure what she *wanted* it to be.

'You don't think taking me down there with you is a risk?' She sent him a sideways look. 'Or do you truly think I'm predictable?'

'I'm very good at taking risks,' he said with no trace of humility. 'And, in my experience, the higher the risk, the greater the reward.'

'So I'm high risk?'

He hesitated, checking his words ever so slightly. 'You're not afraid to put yourself on the line. That makes you interesting.'

She didn't want to be interesting. She didn't want to feel the flush of pleasure that he'd complimented her.

She refused his murmured offer of a drink as they

descended the last stairs. As much as she yearned for the Dutch courage, she figured it would be more of a hindrance than a help. She needed all her wits about her to successfully spar with Alejandro Martinez and combat whatever 'reckoning' it was he had in mind.

Maybe she should have confessed all about the diamond necklace when she had the chance upstairs in the library, but he'd been so irritatingly assured, she'd been unable to resist the urge to bait him right back.

She wasn't sure what she'd expected from him once downstairs, but it wasn't the supremely polite courtesy he showed her. He introduced her to everyone as they walked through the atrium to the formal lounge. Many of them were American, like him, and out to enjoy themselves as much as possible. The first few people he introduced her to looked at her with benign disinterest—clearly used to Alejandro appearing every night with a new woman. No wonder he'd looked bemused when she'd asked what he'd say about her to his guests.

'Meet Catriona,' he said to the fourth group of people they stopped beside.

'Kitty,' she sweetly corrected, yet again, and extended her hand to the nearest of the three women. 'I'm his special date for the night.'

Three sets of eyebrows lifted in unison.

'Special?' one rapier-thin woman queried, her gaze equally dagger-like.

'I had to promise her that, or break out the handcuffs,' Alejandro answered smoothly.

The sensuality of his reply rippled through her—

and the rest of the group. Eyes widened, then narrowed. But only Kitty knew the truth of his words. Only she knew he didn't mean fur-lined kinky toys, but tight, unbreakable restraints—yet somehow the thought of them wasn't as repellent as it should be. Not when she envisaged Alejandro wielding the cuffs and the key.

As Alejandro turned and led her further into the room, the look he sent *her* was slightly goading as if he knew he was thwarting her prediction of his behaviour. As if he knew the lurching direction of her thoughts. She refused to let the smile slip from her face. She'd 'sparkle' down here even if it killed her.

Except it wasn't that hard at all because he made her laugh too easily. He was extremely charming. In minutes she knew exactly why there were so many women present. He had that charisma, that X-factor, that way of looking at a woman as if she were the only person in the world who mattered to him in that moment. When she was the object of his focus, a woman felt *good*. It was a terrifyingly unfair talent. And he shared it around. He had his fingers laced through hers, but he talked with everyone equally.

Then she noticed people were watching them more attentively. Their gazes rested on the way he remained close to her the entire time. At the way he constantly touched some part of her—a hand on her back, her arm, or clasping her hand. As time passed into the second hour, he placed his arm over her shoulder and drew her closer to his side.

The guests began looking more assessingly at *her*. She heard the ripple of inquiry as they made their way from room to room. She heard the whisper of her name. Surreptitious glances became openly speculative.

If Alejandro noticed he said nothing, but his attentiveness became even more apparent. Until he then led her to a corner and stepped in close to put himself as a wall between her and the rest of his guests.

'You seem to be causing a stir,' he said, his onyx gaze pinning her in place.

'Not me.'

He was the one doing all the touchy-feely stuff that was causing the stares.

'Absolutely you.' He laughed. That amusement danced in his eyes too and she couldn't tear her attention from him.

'You enjoy messing with people's lives?'

'In what way am I messing with your life?' He raised his eyebrows. 'Don't overdramatize having to spend one night alongside me. It's not going to change your world.'

'It's not?' She furrowed her brow in mock-disappointment. 'But I thought any woman who spent a night with the amazing Alejandro had her world *rocked*.'

'Minx.' He laughed again. 'Come on, we'd better keep moving.'

'Must we, darling?' she murmured as she stepped alongside him.

The look he shot her then promised absolute retribution.

Kitty lifted her chin, feeling more game than ever. But, now she could look more freely about the house, she realised there was much gone from the rooms. Her family had had a 'maximalist' rather than a 'mini-malist' style of decor but the mantelpieces were bare and shelves barren—the spaces punctuated by used champagne glasses and platters of stupidly tiny deli-cacies she'd yet to sample. With a pang she wondered what he'd done with all the smaller items of furniture and the trinkets and sculptures that she'd loved all her life—surely they weren't all crammed into those boxes in the bedrooms upstairs.

'Alejandro?' a woman called from almost halfway across the room and walked over with quick, clipping steps. 'I've just had a text from Saskia,' she added, her eyes cold and wide as she locked her gaze on Kitty. 'Bit of a bombshell, actually.'

'Oh?' Alejandro couldn't have sounded less inter-ested but his arm tightened infinitesimally, pressing Kitty closer to his side.

She wished he wouldn't do that; feeling his hard strength was appallingly distracting, but she had the feeling he did it without even realising—so used to having a woman with him.

'She said you've met someone else.'

There was a split-second of awkward silence and Alejandro was utterly still. The woman's confident expression suddenly faltered.

'Oh, that would be me,' Kitty interjected sweetly before Alejandro had a chance to speak. 'When I've had enough of him she's welcome to have him back.'

She heard Alejandro's sharply drawn breath and braced herself. Was he finally going to tell her to go now?

But he drew her closer still. It wasn't an unconscious, almost undetectable gesture now. 'But sweet-heart,' he breathed. 'It's my job to ensure you've never had enough.' He turned to the woman. 'If you'll ex-cuse us, I'd like to get Catriona a drink. I think she needs one.'

'How many times do I have to tell you—it's Kitty?' she muttered as he held her hand tightly and drew her through the crowds with him.

He smiled back at her and his hand tightened. 'What will you have?'

She was aware of everyone watching them as he led her through the room. 'Got any cyanide in the champagne?'

'I'll save you some for later, when it's time to face your—how do you say?—fate worse than death.' He looked pleased with himself at that.

'I already told you, that's never happening.'

He stopped in the centre of the room and faced her, apparently uncaring that everyone was staring, and positively *hauled* her right into his arms. 'No? Not even a kiss to say sorry?' Slowly and deliberately he brushed his thumb across her lower lip. 'Methinks the lady doth protest too much.'

'Methinks the asshole doth have an outsize ego.'

He gazed at her, his expression delighted. He couldn't have looked more proprietorial. Or more smitten. But his whispered words were so sarcas-tic and his awareness of her unbelievably smug. He was enjoying her discomfort hugely. She could tell by the unholy gleam in his eyes, but every touch made her acutely aware of him and his magnetism grew stronger.

She pulled back and made him keep walking.

So. Not. Happening.

It was his reputation that made her so aware of him. All that history, the list of conquests—the world's most beautiful, desired women. But it wasn't only that. There was no denying *his* physical perfection and the supreme assuredness that went with it.

It was impossible to look away from him for long. She'd never met anyone like him and she'd met plenty of wealthy, entitled people in the course of her life. But if you were to strip all those people bare of their designer dresses and jewels and outsize bank balances, many would fade into nothingness. Not Alejandro. Buck-naked in a bull ring he'd still conquer all. And she had the feeling he intended to conquer her. He thought he already had.

He had another think coming.

The awareness of the guests was even more apparent now. She felt the heat from a zillion hard gazes and fought to keep the polite smile on her face. She wasn't going to lose her confidence. She was going to keep her head high and weather these last couple of hours. But she was quieter as she stood alongside Alejandro, her hand still firmly bound in his, as he talked work with a couple.

That was when she recognised two of the women on the far side of the room. A small British contingent seemed to be standing together. Kitty's heart sank—of course they'd be there. Those two were like pearl hat pins—ultra pretty but with a sharp point they liked to stick into someone given the chance. She hadn't seen Sarah in months, but she didn't imagine she'd had a personality transplant in that time. The woman was a childhood chum of James's—one who'd never approved of his engagement to Kitty and she was with another couple who were also very much 'team James'. And great, they'd spotted her too and were circling closer like a school of sharks honing in for a feeding frenzy.

'Kitty Parkes-Wilson!' the first exclaimed loudly.

'Hi, Sarah.' Kitty smiled, turning to angle herself slightly away from Alejandro. Given he was engrossed in discussing the prospects of another hedge fund, she crossed her fingers he wouldn't hear this conversation—because if anyone here was going to be predictable, it would be this woman.

'Fancy seeing you here this week of all weeks.' Sure enough, Sarah launched her first salvo in a loud chime.

'You mean in my former family home the week we lost possession?' Kitty smiled through her teeth. 'Funny how life works, isn't it?'

'Oh, it is,' Sarah answered as she glanced at Alejandro's hand curling around Kitty's despite the fact he was facing the other couple. 'I never thought you'd be another of Alejandro's notches,' she 'whispered' conspiratorially.

'I'm not!' Kitty flared at the thought and replied swiftly before thinking better of it. 'I'm only here because he's bullied me into staying.'

Sarah's eyebrows lifted and she laughed a little too loudly. 'Bullied?' Her pointed laugh chimed loudly again. 'Yeah, it really looks like that.'

Was it Kitty's imagination or had Alejandro tensed?

'We haven't seen you in so long,' Sarah added

when Kitty didn't elaborate. 'You left London in such a hurry.'

The woman was such a cow to bring that up. Of course she'd left in a hurry. She'd been *hurt*. She'd just found out James hadn't wanted *her* at all. He'd only wanted the wealth he'd assumed came with her. And when he'd found out all the cold hard cash had gone, he hadn't bothered to break up with her before searching the field for her replacement. He'd been trying them all out behind her back. Now, barely six months later, he was engaged to another woman. A beautiful, wealthy one who didn't seem at all bothered about his cheating past.

This time Kitty didn't imagine the sensation. Alejandro's fingers definitely tightened about hers again. But he didn't break his conversation and turn towards her.

'You're finally over James then?' Sarah queried.

She knew it hadn't been her fault, but it still hurt. She'd truly thought he loved her. That he'd got her, and found her attractive. But it was only the money he'd loved. And she'd been so starved for attention, so desperate to believe that a guy finally wanted *her*, she'd not seen through his fickle facade.

She'd been such a fool. And she was a fool now for letting this woman get to her.

Because she was too angry.

She straightened, channelled her inner Great-Aunt Margot and rewrote the rules.

'Oh, yes.' Kitty smiled sunnily at Sarah. 'You know, I didn't want to make things public yet,' she 'whispered'—every bit as loudly as Sarah had. 'As you've alluded to, it has been a stressful week.'

Sarah's eyes widened and she leaned closer. 'Make what public?' This time her volume really did lower.

'Our relationship,' Kitty answered as if it was obvious.

'Your...' Sarah's jaw slackened in shock, then she almost squeaked. 'You mean with Alejandro? *You're* why he bought this house? He bought it for you?'

It was amazing how the smallest suggestion could snowball into something so out of control so quickly.

'It's a secret, you understand,' Kitty murmured guiltily, not quite correcting Sarah's assumption and hoping Alejandro was still deeply involved with his conversation and not eavesdropping.

'The two of you are that...*serious*?' Sarah's voice rose.

She was so obviously thunderstruck at the notion that Kitty was suddenly irate. Why was it so shocking that an attractive man might want *her*? Just for once she wanted to knock the superior smirk from this woman's face—and every other person who'd looked at her as if she were a loser freak. 'We're—'

Sarah's eyes narrowed on the way Alejandro was holding Kitty's left hand so firmly. 'You're *never* engaged,' she breathed.

'We're...er...' Kitty suddenly realised a metaphorical crevasse had opened at her feet. She was in real trouble.

That was when Alejandro turned.

If only the earth really would open up and swallow her whole.

'Kitty's just told me the news.' Sarah reached out and put a hand on his wrist and shot Kitty a sharp

look before Kitty could even draw breath. 'Congratulations.'

Kitty couldn't bring herself to look at him.

And then Sarah did it. She asked so loudly that
several heads turned. 'Are you two really engaged,
Alejandro?'

CHAPTER THREE

ALEJANDRO'S FINGERS TIGHTENED again on Kitty's—
extremely firmly.

But Kitty didn't wince. She held her breath, waiting for the ultimate in public humiliation. It was suddenly so quiet, it was as if the rest of the world was
holding its breath with her. This would actually be
worse than when she'd finally found out about James's
infidelity. At least she'd been alone then and not in
the centre of a roomful of people.

'Sarah guessed,' Kitty muttered as she finally
braved a glance up at him and recklessly killed the silence that had been a fraction too long already. 'She's
always been astute.'

His gaze imprisoned hers and for a second everyone in the room faded. His eyes were like banked fur-
naces, so very black but so very deep and there was a
level of emotion in them that she'd not expected and
that she couldn't interpret.

Oh, God, she should just run away now.

His fingers tightened even more—to the point of
pain—as if he'd read her mind and was physically
preventing her escape. But she wanted to run. She
had to. How could she ever explain?

Sarah—the one who'd never told her that her fiancé was sleeping with someone else. Sarah—who'd never been nice, who'd never welcomed her into the group, who'd never seemed to want her to succeed.

'You've caught her out, Sarah,' Alejandro said quietly.

Kitty started to die inside.

'Catriona was reluctant to announce it so soon...' He trailed off.

Sarah's jaw dropped. So did Kitty's, but she caught herself in time. She licked her lips, her heart thundering as she gazed at Alejandro. He was smiling? He was looking...*satisfied*?

He turned to face her nemesis intently. 'We can trust you, can't we?'

'Of course,' Sarah said weakly. 'But I...er...might have been a bit loud just then.'

'No matter.' Alejandro smiled. 'We're all friends here.'

Did he underline the word 'friends'? He still held Kitty's hand in a vice but he was smiling.

'Congratulations.' Sarah looked stunned.

Alejandro lifted his free hand to place a finger over his lips and winked at her. 'Shh, remember?' Finally he turned to Kitty again. 'Come along, Catriona. I think you need some fresh air.'

He set off at such a pace Kitty almost stumbled. If it weren't for the grip he had on her hand, she might have. Instead he wrapped his other arm around her waist and—under the guise of attentive affection—practically dragged her out through the back room, past that bland dishwashing guy and out into the small private courtyard at the back.

Only once they were alone outside did he release her. Kitty took a quick few steps to the corner of the tiled courtyard. Then turned to face him.

'We're engaged?' He sent her a look.

With the bright lights gleaming from the house, this one was easy to interpret. He was *amused*?

'It's your fault,' she declared, instantly defensive. 'I was trying not to be predictable. You dared me.'

'So it's *my* fault?'

'This entire mess is your fault.' She nodded firmly.

He slowly stepped closer. 'You don't feel any responsibility, given you're the one who broke in and tried to steal from me?'

'I didn't break in; I used a key. And I wasn't stealing anything that belongs to you.'

'No? I wonder.' He was watching her closely, then his smile returned, slow and seductive. 'Catriona, you are going to pay for this, you know.'

'Not in the way you're thinking.'

He laughed and stepped so he was right in her personal space. 'Very much in the way I'm thinking. You think these sparks can be ignored?'

She really wished his accent didn't make his atrocious words sound so damn attractive. His laugh was low and did things to her insides and the cool air did nothing to settle the fever in her bones.

Now she really wished he'd stop looking at her like that. It made her hot and it was even harder to concentrate. And he knew it. He knew he was like catnip to every woman in the world. He loved it. She didn't want to want him at all. But her stupid body recognised the talent and experience in his.

'Is this the bit where you attempt to exert your sexual dominance over me?' she growled as he stepped closer still.

He let out another burst of laughter, but he caught both her hands in his and forced them behind her back in a move of total sexual dominance. 'No, this is the bit where I stop you from saying more stupid things in public.'

'You have no right to censor me.' She had no idea where the wildness came from. She'd never normally speak to anyone like this. Usually she'd duck her head and mind her own business and let Teddy do the talking.

'Not censoring you,' he chided wickedly. 'Kissing you. To leave you speechless.'

'You're...*what*?' Her jaw dropped. 'You're unbelievable.'

'I know. So good.' He mock preened.

But his proximity was getting to her—she could feel his strength and his size and, appallingly, she wanted to lean up against him! She stiffened instead. 'You don't think you're hyping yourself up too much? I'm going to expect something so amazing you're never going to be able to live up to it.'

'I'm willing to take the risk.'

'You're willing to take a lot of risks.'

'Possibly. But this is my home and you will not cause trouble when I have this many guests present.'

'Then let me leave. With my necklace.' She looked up and sent him a brilliant smile, pleased with her comeback. 'It's a very simple solution.'

'No, that can't happen now,' he answered bluntly, his expression intent. 'Stupid talk earns kissing, remember?'

Kitty didn't get the chance to breathe, let alone reply. Because he'd bent his head and brushed his lips over hers. It was the softest, lightest kiss and not at all what she'd have expected. Silenced, stilled, she waited. There was another light, gentle caress—lips on lips. And then another.

That was when she realised he was the kind of lover who would take his time. Infinite time and care, to arouse her. The thing was, she didn't need that much time. Her toes curled in the ends of her shoes as he kissed her again and she couldn't help her slight gasp, the parting of her suddenly needy mouth. But he didn't press closer, harder—instead, he kept the kiss light, almost sweet, and he was utterly in control. There was just that underlying edge as she absorbed the rigidity of his body…and started to realise that the tightness of his grasp on her wrists was no longer to hold her in place, but to hold himself back.

She looked up at him, bemused by his tender, go softly approach. He threw her a small smile, as if he knew exactly how much she'd anticipated a punishing kiss from him—all frantic passion and a duelling race to the finish line.

And she was *not* disappointed it hadn't become that kind of kiss. Nor was she yearning for another.

'That wasn't enough?' he teased knowingly. 'You want a little more?'

'That was more than enough,' she lied with a little shrug. 'I guess this is where you say we English have no passion.'

'I've yet to meet a woman who doesn't feel passion when she's with me—'

'You mean anger? Rage?'

He chuckled and brushed his thumb across her hyper-sensitised lips. 'Too easy.'

Awareness rippled down her spine, a warm tide of liquid desire. It was impossible that she be so drawn to this man. He was a philanderer—a total playboy who'd had more lovers than she had freckles. And she had a *lot* of freckles.

He was just toying with her—too aware of his sensual power and utterly assured of his success.

'I won't be another of your numbers.' She promised herself that.

'No?' He laughed and shook her gently. 'You already are. More than that—you're my fiancée.'

She died of mortification all over again. In the heat of that kiss she'd forgotten that nightmare moment. 'Why didn't you deny it?' She swallowed.

'I don't like seeing anyone ganged up on,' he said simply. 'I dislike bullies. It was evident what was going on.'

What would the supremely successful Alejandro Martinez know about bullies? As she frowned at him another emotion flickered across his face. But he suddenly stepped back, looking as suavely in control as ever. He extended his hand to her and waited. That he was so astute surprised her. Now she knew why he hadn't denied that outrageous engagement story to Sarah. He'd felt *sorry* for her. She felt worse than ever.

She hesitated, looking into his eyes, unable to read him at all now.

'Let's go back inside,' he said quietly.

With a small sigh she put her hand in his and walked

back into the house. But they didn't return to the packed ground floor reception rooms; instead he led her up the stairs that she had previously used to get to the private library.

'Stay here awhile, make yourself at home,' he teased wolfishly as he showed her into the room.

She should have known that moment of kindness and humanity wouldn't last in him.

'Where are you going?' She eyed him suspiciously.

He had his phone out and a key in his hand—one of the large old-fashioned keys that fitted the internal doors in this house.

'I'm going to get rid of all my guests. I can do that better if you're not with me.'

'And you're going to lock me in here while you do that?' She folded her arms and called him on it. 'What if there's a fire?'

'I'll play the hero and rescue you.' He simply smiled and looked rakish.

'You're no hero—you're all villain.'

He flashed another smile. 'Women always like the bad boy, isn't that so?'

That was *not* so. She felt like flinging the cushions at him, except she wasn't that childish. Guiltily she remembered her lies downstairs. She'd definitely acted like a proud, childish idiot then.

'Don't fret.' He winked at her just before closing—and locking—the door. 'I won't be long.'

He was an inordinately long time. Eventually she heard voices spilling out into the street and resisted the urge to stand at the window and scream for a saviour. She'd made enough of a fool of herself here tonight. What had she been thinking when she'd led

Sarah to think Alejandro had bought the house for her? That they were *engaged*?

Tired defeat permeated her. She'd been up since six, ready to get the train from Cornwall back to London. She'd not eaten on the journey and now she felt queasy. She turned off the main light and switched on the reading lamp, pouring herself a finger of whiskey from the decanter still on the table in the study.

She rarely drank spirits but right now she needed *something* and she trusted her father's old single malt more than the concoctions that had been on offer downstairs. And, anyway, this was for medicinal purposes. The liquid hit her stomach and lit a ball of fire in it. She breathed out and closed her eyes, aching to relax properly. She'd spark up again when Alejandro returned. She just needed a bit of a rest now.

The heat drained from her. That kick of adrenalin vanished, leaving her tired and with a headache threatening. She kicked off her shoes and walked to the deep leather sofa that had been in her father's study all her life, trying not to remember the number of times she'd curled up on it and waited late into the night for him to get home.

She'd spent so long trying to get her father's attention. But he'd been preoccupied lecturing Teddy, the son and heir, and he'd been too busy wooing the glamorous women he'd had affairs with. She'd gifted him her best sculptures as a kid. She'd poured her heart into them, only to see them admired for a half second and then relegated to a bottom shelf to gather dust. They were never properly displayed, never shown off with pride, merely indulged for a brief moment before he turned elsewhere. Which was exactly the way he treated *her*.

All she'd wanted was for him to know her, to love her, to let her *be*… She was such a needy fool.

She'd thought James had understood and that he'd be true to her. But he'd been even worse. At least her father had never hidden his affairs from everyone.

'I was just… I couldn't help myself.' Her father had tried to explain it to her the last time she'd seen him, just after she'd broken up with James, and she'd railed at him for being the same kind of *cheat*.

Impulse. Making that snap decision that was so often wrong. She'd inherited that faulty gene from him. Not when it came to lovers, but in every other aspect of her life for sure.

Her father had made bad business choices; he'd needed to sell property to get a cash injection because he'd known his time as a businessman was up. He'd wanted to retire to his flash estate in Corsica while he still could. And so he had. Leaving Teddy and her alone. But they were almost twenty-four and able to look after themselves.

Now she was exhausted from maintaining smiles in front of all those people. From restraining herself from losing her temper with Alejandro in front of them all. From reining in her reaction to the torment of his touches. From hiding the heartbreak at being back here and knowing she no longer belonged. That she'd never really belonged. There was nothing here for her any more.

She curled her legs under her on the sofa and told herself to shrug it off. She was fine. She'd go and stay with Teddy at one of his friends' places tonight after having it out with Alejandro. She'd go back to Cornwall in the morning and get on with her new life. It was all going to be okay.

But in the meantime she slumped lower in the soft leather.

It took longer than Alejandro desired for his guests to get the idea it was time for them to leave. Admittedly his parties usually went on far later, but he needed to be alone with the vexatious redhead who'd tipped his night upside down. So he smiled, firmly shooting down the teasing pleas for the DJ to play on.

Finally he closed the door on the last couple of guests, who were still shocked and avidly curious. Yeah, that 'friend' of Catriona's hadn't kept her mouth shut. But he'd known she wouldn't. They'd all known that.

Rolling his shoulders to ease the tension mounting in them, he lightly jogged up the stairs. His smile was tight. She was going to be furious with him for taking so long. But when he unlocked the door he wasn't greeted with the instant volley of verbal abuse he'd expected. His breath froze in his lungs at the total silence in the room. Had she escaped somehow? He strode into the library then drew up short—the sight before him rendered him speechless. He simply stared.

She was fast asleep on the sofa, her body a sleek, long shadow of woman. Her skin shone pale in the soft light, but her hair was a riot of flames cascading about her face and shoulders. God, she was beautiful. Different. Sexy as hell.

Desire ripped through him—igniting a fierce animal

urge to wake her, kiss her, claim her body with his, here and now. The longing to feel her beneath him was sudden and acute. He clenched his fists at the ferocity of the ache and forced himself to take a calming breath.

No. *No.*

He never wanted any woman as intensely as all that. He never felt *anything* as intensely as all that. He refused. He had reason to.

He breathed deeply again and reminded himself of his rational decisions. He hadn't been going to *make* her stay the night—despite the teasing and the incredibly erotic pleasure of her kiss. He'd been planning to get to the bottom of the necklace situation and then say goodbye to her, hadn't he?

But now here she was with her shoes off, fast asleep on the old sofa. He guessed it wasn't the first time she'd slept on it.

He frowned as he quietly stepped closer to study her. He hadn't seen just how pale she was earlier, or noticed those smudges under her eyes. She looked exhausted.

'Catriona?' he softly called to her. 'Kitty?'

She didn't stir. He'd known she wouldn't. She was in too deep a sleep. Something twisted inside Alejandro as he understood how vulnerable she was in this moment and the degree to which he was entrusted with her *care*. An icy droplet snaked down his spine. This was a complication he hadn't foreseen and didn't particularly want. Maintaining the care and wellbeing of another was not his forte. But he fetched a blanket from his room and covered her to make her more comfortable until she woke of her own accord. He hoped she would soon.

He sat in the large armchair opposite the sofa and pulled the necklace from his pocket to inspect it properly in the lamplight. It was definitely worth serious money and she'd risked a lot to get it back. But it wasn't hers.

Over the years, so many of those wealthy people he'd studied alongside had annoyed him when they'd shown a lack of appreciation of how damn lucky they were. He'd never taken his success or his security for granted. How could he when he'd come from worse than nothing? So he'd worked harder than any of them. Ensured his grades were the best. Swinging from one scholarship to the next, climbing higher and higher out of a life of poverty, misery, desperation. And his 'party lifestyle' that claimed all the headlines was but a tiny fraction of his time. The rest was spent working. Still working. Still achieving. Still ensuring success. And now a spoilt young woman had waltzed in to reclaim—what—her inheritance? The wealth she'd never had to earn for herself.

She'd been brazen and bold in her initial dismissal of him, outrageous in the reckless way she'd back-chatted him, and he'd fully planned to teach her a thing or two. Except he'd then heard the tone in which that other woman had spoken to her and there'd been no mistaking it. He hated bullies— whether they were the kind who used vicious words or the violent fists he'd experienced. So he hadn't shamed her publicly. He'd backed her and there'd been no missing the bright relief in her eyes. But then her nerve in the private courtyard when she'd insisted it was all *his* fault? When he'd given in to that urge to kiss her?

He glanced at his Sleeping Beauty again—remembering the softness of her lips, the stirring in her muscles…the *spark*. He couldn't regret that—no matter the complication that now arose.

But now he was stuck with the story that she and he were engaged. He'd smiled his way through the shocked shouts of congratulations from every one of his guests as he'd ushered them out. He'd explained that Catriona had been overwhelmed by the attention and that they'd have another party soon. It was ridiculous but he hadn't been able to find it within himself to reveal the truth. He'd seen that vulnerability when she'd looked at him. He'd seen that hurt. It echoed within him. Didn't he know what it was like to be that isolated? And afraid.

She was a contrary mix of assertiveness and insecurity, a bit broken but bluffing anyway. He liked that spirit. And he wanted her.

Well, if he was going to have her, he was going to have to play it carefully. She obviously wasn't someone who went from affair to affair.

He felt the vibration again and quietly extracted her phone from his pocket. He didn't want to wake her yet, not when she was so obviously wiped out, but it seemed someone was concerned for her welfare. The name 'Teddy' was written across the screen and the photo beneath the lettering was of the two of them. The resemblance was impossible to miss. The man was blond rather than red-haired, but he shared the same smile, the same shaped eyes. He had to be her brother.

Alejandro didn't answer the call; rather he put the phone on the wide arm of the chair he was sitting in and picked up his own phone. A simple Internet search was all it took to remind himself of the family details. Teddy—Edward—and Kitty—Catriona—Parkes-Wilson were the twin children of the man he'd bought this house from. He entered another search and soon enough came up with a photo of an elderly woman—Margot Parkes—wearing the diamond choker Kitty had come here to collect.

And then there were the pictures of Kitty herself. It seemed she was something of an artist—a sculptor. She'd had a few mentions in the society pages; there was the announcement of an engagement to some man named James that hadn't lasted. Another reason to take care with her. But Alejandro was confident; his affairs always ended easily and well and maybe something light and sexual was exactly what the woman needed. Something fun—he did fun really well.

There were more mentions of her brother. And then there was the item about Alejandro's purchase of Parkes House. Apparently it had been in her family for generations. He didn't feel bad about the transaction. He'd paid more than a fair price and if businesses failed, they failed. He'd needed a London base and he'd got one.

When her phone rang for the tenth time he finally relented, feeling only the smallest sympathy for the man who'd allowed his sister to put herself at such risk for his sake.

He touched the screen to take the call. Teddy spoke before Alejandro had the chance to say hello.

'Kitty? For God's sake, are you okay? Did you get the diamonds?'

'I'm sorry, Teddy,' Alejandro replied calmly. 'Both your sister and the diamonds are with me.'

CHAPTER FOUR

KITTY OPENED HER EYES, blinking at the bright light streaming in through the gap in the heavy brocade curtains. She frowned as she took in the familiar surroundings. She was in the second floor library on her father's sofa—

She froze as it all came flooding back. Alejandro Martinez now owned Parkes House. He'd coerced her into being his date. He'd kissed her. He'd said they'd have a reckoning and here she was, waking the next *day*—

'Good morning.'

She sat up quickly, clutching the soft woollen blanket to her, taking a split second to realise she was still fully clothed. Then she looked up, gaping as he took a seat in the armchair opposite. For a moment all she could do was stare. He looked even more striking in the daylight. So gorgeously striking.

Then she snapped herself together.

'What happened?' Warily she brushed her hair back from her face and shifted so she was sitting up properly, her feet on the floor ready to run.

'You fell asleep while I was getting rid of the other

guests,' he said easily. 'You've been out for hours; I was starting to get concerned.'

Kitty's skipping pulse didn't settle. He must've showered not that long ago because his hair was still damp and now he wore jeans and a white tee, but he looked no less wolfish than he had the night before. No less to-die-for.

Half her innards melted. She loathed her reaction to him. How superficial could she get? Wowed by chiselled cheekbones, a fit body and a cockier-than-hell attitude.

In that instant he smiled at her as if he knew exactly what she was thinking.

'I have a proposition for you,' he said.

'I already said no thank you,' she said primly. *Determinedly.*

He gestured to a mug of coffee on the low table beside her. Steam curled in the light. 'I'm guessing you like it strong and unsweetened.'

Clearly she *was* that predictable after all. 'Why do you think that?'

'You're a starving artist who needs to make the most of every drop she gets.'

Silently she reached out for the coffee. He'd been doing some research.

'I made your father an offer he couldn't refuse,' he said. 'I'll make you one too.'

'My father didn't much care for this place anyway,' Kitty muttered and drank the coffee. She needed to kick-start her grey matter. 'He thought it was cold.'

'It is cold,' Alejandro said dryly. 'I've ordered a new heating system.'

Because he had the bajillions required to maintain and upgrade a heritage building like this one. She knew it was petty, but she hated him for that. He had no idea of the history of this house.

'But you like this building.' He smiled when she didn't answer. 'I can tell by the way you look around it. Listen to my offer.'

'I'll refuse anything you offer me,' she said fiercely. She wouldn't be bought as easily as her father had been. She'd never say yes to this man.

Now she remembered the humiliation of Sarah being here last night and seeing her. And the story she'd spun—that they were *engaged*? Oh, hell, the sooner she ran back to Cornwall the better.

'Maybe.' He smiled. 'But you might not want to. Why not hear me out first and then decide?'

He stood and walked over to the desk and returned with a large platter. Kitty looked at the freshly sliced fruit and pastries and swallowed to stop herself drooling. She was *starving*.

'Go ahead and eat,' Alejandro commented lazily. 'It'll make you feel better.'

She restrained herself from sending him a stabbing glance. He might be right, but he didn't need to sound so patronising.

'What's your ever so fabulous offer?' she asked, reaching for the fruit.

He watched as she bit into the pineapple before replying and for a moment Kitty wouldn't have heard or understood a word he said anyway. She was famished—and this fruit was so fresh it was all she could do to stop herself devouring it all in two seconds flat.

She heard his low chuckle and he sat back in the chair and pulled the diamond choker from his pocket.

'Tell me about this,' he said.

She gazed sadly at the coil of glittering stones in his hand but shook her head.

'You think you're protecting someone?' His eyebrows lifted. 'I know it belongs to your brother.'

He *had* been doing his research. 'Yes.'

'But you're the one who loves it.'

She bristled at the hint of censure. Did he think she was a materialistic, do-anything-for-diamonds kind of girl? 'I loved the woman it originally belonged to,' she said haughtily. 'I love what the diamonds symbolise, not what they're worth. They have irreplaceable *sentimental* value.'

His frown hadn't lessened. 'So why do they belong to your brother?'

She sighed. 'Because he's the firstborn and the boy.'

Now a baffled look crossed his face. 'Are we still in the Middle Ages?'

'*You're* the one who forced me to be your date last night, so I'd say I'm currently living in the Neanderthal era. Barbaric caveman,' she muttered beneath her breath.

'Poor baby.' His smile flashed and he leaned back in his seat, oozing sensual confidence. 'So what are you willing to do to get your necklace back?'

'Not that.' She picked up a *pain au chocolat* and chomped on it.

'I'm not that crass. We'll sleep together only when you've grown up enough to admit how much you want to.'

He laughed at her expression. His arrogance knew no bounds.

But then he sobered. 'You didn't think that you could have just contacted my lawyer? Or perhaps knocked on the front door and asked me politely? Explained there was a mix-up?'

Was that a glimpse of hurt in his eyes? Surely not.

'Am I such a monster you had to resort to breaking the law to get what belonged to your family?'

Kitty finally managed to swallow the lump of concrete masquerading as pastry in her mouth. 'You're the one who admitted to doing whatever necessary to get what you want. At the time I thought this was necessary.'

'Fair enough, but you know there are consequences to your actions. All your actions.'

'You're calling the police?'

'You should be so lucky.' His smile this time wasn't so nice. 'No, if you want the necklace back, then you make amends.'

'How do you want me to do that?'

'You fulfil the role you claimed last night. You be my fiancée.'

'*What?*'

Calmly he put the choker back into his pocket and then shot her a look. 'You remain here as my fiancée for a few weeks until we amicably break up and then you leave.'

'Why would you want me to do that?'

'Because it suits me.'

'And it's all about you.'

'Right now, yes, it is.' He shrugged. 'You broke

into my house. You spread stories about me to all my friends. I think you owe me.'

She felt guilty enough already; she didn't need him laying it on with a trowel.

'I'm opening up the London office of my company,' he went on. 'It's a big investment and I don't want this sideshow overshadowing or impacting on its success. It doesn't need to be a big deal; interest will fade very quickly once the company set-up is fully underway.'

'I can't just stay here as your fiancée. I have a job.'

'You have a part-time position in a failing art gallery in the south of England where you don't actually get paid; you merely get a roof over your head and use of the small studio out the back.'

Yes, he'd done a *lot* of research. She'd gone to Cornwall on a whim when her engagement to James had ended in that blaze of exposure and humiliation. She'd been there for the last six months. Happy enough, but lonely. She'd been unable to resist Teddy's call for help.

'It's not failing,' she grumbled, just so she could fight with him about something. 'It's a beautiful gallery. The light down there is amazing.'

'I want you to work here and catalogue everything in this mausoleum. There are things in piles of boxes that I haven't the time to open and sift through.'

'So you can auction it off and make money from every little thing?'

'I don't need the money from these trinkets. They'd add less than a drop to my financial ocean.'

Oh, please—bully for him for being so wealthy. 'I could steal from you, you know.'

'I'm willing to take that risk.' He smiled.

'Don't you have ten personal assistants or something?'

'My PA is extremely efficient and I'm sure she'd do a good job, but her talents are better spent on the work she knows best. It's better for this to be done by someone familiar with the content. The place is in a mess and you know it.'

He was right and it wasn't just the boxes; there were years of repairs that had been left undone. Like his business, her father had left the house in a mess.

'It needs an upgrade, and you can make the arrangements, at least for the chattels to begin with. A full restoration programme will take much longer, of course.' Alejandro regarded her steadily. 'So what do you think?'

She thought it was a flimsy excuse to keep her here just because…he simply wanted it. And he always got what he wanted, that was obvious. Yet his plan appealed to the spot where she was most vulnerable. She'd loved this home and she wanted to save some of those things. 'So you're not going to modernise, but restore?'

'The building has many beautiful features that I find attractive and would like to keep.' He nodded. 'Of course I want to see it restored to its glory—not just the shell, but the interior as well.'

She felt her flush of gratitude mounting. It was so stupid, but he'd got her there. And he knew it.

'You have an understanding of the items that are here; you can assess their value and importance. Catalogue them with a sell or keep recommendation and I'll make my decision when I have time.'

She thought about it for a long moment. It was so tempting, but it was also impossible. And insane. She shook her head. 'I can't go from one engagement to another.'

Not even to a fake one.

'It's been about six months, hasn't it?' Alejandro pointed out, lazily selecting one of the grapes she'd left behind on the platter.

'Who have you been talking to?' She was mortified that he knew of her past.

He swallowed the fruit and laughed. 'What does it matter?' He reached forward, his teasing expression back. 'You know a rebound romance is the perfect solution for that bad temper.'

'This will never be a *romance*,' she snarled, shocked at the way she was suddenly burning up.

'No?' He looked amused. 'I was trying to make it sound less…raw.'

'Less tacky, you mean.' He was talking about lust and nothing but.

'You need a system cleanse.' He lifted his hands in that unexpectedly animated way that made her want to smile back at him. 'A little light fun to restore your confidence and independence.'

'And you're offering?' Like the generous, do-good kind of guy he so wasn't. 'A little light fun?'

What, exactly, would that entail? And why was it suddenly so hot in here?

'I'm offering many things. All of them good.' Still leaning forward, he propped his chin in his hand as he watched her. 'You don't have anywhere else to stay in London at the moment. I believe your brother is between apartments as well.'

Oh, hell, he knew it all. And the truth was, the prospect of couch-surfing with Teddy's theatre friends for the next few days was depressing. Her father hadn't thought it necessary to consider whether she'd have a place to stay. And nor should he. She was twenty-three and perfectly capable of finding her own accommodation. But she hadn't realised how adrift she really was. 'Is there *anything* you don't know?'

'There are many things I don't know about you. Yet.'

The implied intimacy brought more colour to her cheeks.

'It is the organisation of the house that earns you back the diamonds,' he said. 'Our sexual relationship is outside of that bargain.'

'We have no sexual relationship,' she said firmly.

'Yet,' he repeated with a smile. 'It's only a matter of time, Catriona.'

'Not everything is that predictable.'

'This is.'

She drew in a shallow breath. 'And if I refuse to organise the house?'

'No necklace.'

'But it's not yours. It wasn't part of the house sale and you know it.'

'As you said yourself, possession is nine-tenths of the law. I have it, Catriona.' He patted his pocket. 'I'll tell the world about your attempt to break in and steal from me. That initially I covered for you last night to spare your mortification, but that in the end you had to be charged.'

'Wouldn't that bring the "sideshow" you're so keen

to avoid?' she asked, delighting in pointing out his own contradiction.

He shrugged. 'I would prefer to avoid that, but I've been through worse. I'm not the villain in this—*you're* the crazy woman.'

She was. She'd be labelled the desperate woman who'd faked a fiancé to save face. Humiliation sucked. This was a way of escaping with some pride intact. And it wasn't all beneficence on his part; she knew what he wanted and frankly she was amazed—and stupidly flattered. She wasn't anything like the beautiful, curvy models he dated.

The sound of a phone ringing startled her. Even more so when she realised it was *her* phone ringing.

Alejandro took her phone from his other pocket and tossed it to her, his gaze alert and speculative. 'You'd better answer this time. He keeps ringing.'

She glanced at the screen. Teddy. He'd be having conniptions.

'Kitty? You're still in his house?' her brother said as soon as she answered.

So Alejandro had spoken to Teddy. No wonder he knew about the diamonds and everything else. Her brother couldn't keep a secret if he tried.

'How did he catch you?' Teddy's astonishment rang down the phone the second she answered. 'You got in and out so many times over the years and *never* got caught.'

Mainly because no one had cared enough to notice if she was missing. 'Well, I did this time.' The guy had to have eyes like a hawk. There'd been so many people present, she never should have been spotted.

'Well, there's the most preposterous story going

around. My phone's been ringing flat-out. Everyone thinks you've been seeing him in secret all this time. They're saying you're *engaged*.'

'Oh, hell…' She covered her face with her hand. She'd made the most colossal fool of herself.

She peeked through her fingers and saw Alejandro had sat back more comfortably in his chair and was smiling, as if enjoying her mortification. She realised then that he was waiting for her to decide. That maybe he didn't actually care that much either way.

'So it's not true?'

She heard the disappointment in her brother's voice. And the anxious edge. She didn't want Teddy to worry or try to come charging in here and sorting it out and making it all even more embarrassing. Maybe this situation could be resolved best if the details were kept between her and the devil in front of her. Between *only* them. She'd suffer this mortification in front of Alejandro alone.

'They're saying he stepped in to save Dad's cash flow because he's been in love with you all this time,' Teddy said.

She laughed a little hysterically. 'Oh, Teddy, it's not quite that simple.'

'But you *are* his fiancée?'

She hesitated, glancing up to meet Alejandro's penetrating gaze for a long moment.

'Kitty…' Teddy's voice lowered. 'Are you okay? When I phoned last night he was very short with me.'

'Everything's fine, Teddy.' She tore her gaze from Alejandro's, straightened her shoulders and made herself smile. 'They're more than fine. But things are a little…complicated—'

'I didn't think you even knew him. Last night you were—' He broke off almost as soon as he'd interrupted. 'Shit, is that why you were in such a hurry to get there?'

'Look, I'll come and see you in a couple of days, okay? I'll explain it then. But for now I am staying here.'

'*With* him?' Teddy's excitement barrelled down the phone. 'You're really staying with him?'

'Yes.'

It took almost a full minute after ending the call with Teddy before she could lift her chin and look Alejandro in the face again. She was just waiting for him to gloat with some smart comment. But when she did look at him, she found he was watching her with just the smallest of smiles. It wasn't even a smug one.

'At least here you can have a bed,' he offered blandly.

'My own bed?'

'Of course, until you ask to share mine.'

'Not going to happen.'

He laughed then. 'You're too constricted by your own naivety,' he jeered. 'Believing in some fairy tale version of romance and being in a relationship " happily-ever-after".'

'You don't believe in relationships?' Why wasn't she surprised?

'Not lasting ones.' His smile flashed.

'So not marriage.'

'Definitely not. I will never marry.'

'That's sad,' she said glibly.

'What's sad is the vast number of people who stay in unhappy marriages because they think they have to.' He shrugged carelessly. 'I like indulging—in nice food, pleasant company, good sex. Then a gentle goodbye. What's wrong with that?' He breathed it with utter confidence and arrogance.

'Nothing.' She couldn't fault him for what seemed to be the perfect life. For him. Because she didn't think the goodbye Saskia had got had been all that gentle.

'I work hard. I achieve. I get what I deserve.'

'I hope you do,' she said pointedly.

He didn't look remotely abashed. 'The women I tend to date have worked every bit as hard as I have to achieve their successes.'

'With plastic surgery and liberal use of the casting couch,' she muttered.

'You judge your sisters so harshly?'

She wrinkled her nose, hating that he was right and she'd been bitchy.

'I treat all my lovers with respect and courtesy,' he said meaningfully. 'A little kindness goes a long way.'

'But you have no desire to be faithful?'

His eyes widened. 'I sleep with one woman at a time. I don't date another until I have ensured anyone else I had been seeing is clear that we are no longer an item.'

As he'd done with poor Saskia.

'Is that what you'll do with me if we have an affair? Just flick me a text before jumping into bed with another woman?'

Her cheeks heated. James hadn't done even that. He'd cheated on her.

'We will formally end our engagement. There will be no miscommunication or misunderstanding.'

'And now you think I should just fall into bed with you?'

'I think if you were honest about what you want, that's exactly what you'd do.' He watched her closely. 'There's nothing wrong with lust, Catriona.'

Maybe there wasn't, but she wasn't ready for it. And not for him. 'Okay, here's some honesty for you,' she said, trying to take control of the situation and clarify her intentions. 'You're an attractive man and you know it. But we don't share the same desires. I don't want that kind of empty pleasure. I want something more meaningful and complicated. So I'll do the house. I'll stay until this stupid story blows over. But that's all. And when that's done, then I go.'

He was not winning. He was not getting everything his own way. She'd be his first failure.

'You think you can resist this chemistry?' He grinned, hugely amused. 'Are you one of those women who has to believe she's in love before she'll have sex with a man?'

'Not love necessarily. But something a little warmer than loathing.'

He laughed and stood. 'I will not muddy this affair with false declarations or meaningless promises. When you want me, just let me know.'

'I'll send you a telegram.' She blew him a kiss. 'Now, go to work, darling, so I can steal from you while your back is turned.'

Alejandro knew he could have her far sooner than she pretended. Knew that it would take only a few kisses and she'd be heavy-eyed and restless in his arms, as she'd been for those too brief moments last night. But now he wanted more than that from her.

Now he'd seen her defiant rise to his challenge, the determined denial sparking in her eyes. That spirit and courage showed she wasn't so much broken as bruised. He'd help her forget the stupid ex-fiancé.

But he wanted her to hit the ignition on their affair. To be unable to deny this chemistry without his provocation. He didn't know why. Usually he wasn't that bothered—either he took a lover or he didn't. It was straightforward. But Catriona presented a challenge that he couldn't resist engaging with. Maybe some old-fashioned seduction was required, until the electricity was too high a voltage to be ignored and she came to him.

He'd worked like a demon this morning to arrange everything. He'd sent his assistant to stay in a hotel for the week. He'd be at work most of the time, but when he was here he didn't want anyone interrupting him and Catriona. It struck him that things might get fiery at any moment. He was looking forward to that. And, with her unconventional beauty, she fitted in this house. The fact she could help with excavating all the residual stuff that was seemingly cemented inside it was pure bonus.

'I'm happy to have you as my fiancée for the foreseeable future,' he said, pleased with the outcome.

It was the perfect solution. He got someone to sort the house and he'd get to sleep with the most vexingly sexy woman he'd encountered in a while.

'I'm not staying here for long.' She suddenly looked uneasy.

Was she attempting to back out of the deal already? Because she knew she wasn't going to win?

He smothered his smile. 'Why not? The house is big; there's a lot of rubbish to get rid of.'

'It's not rubbish—' Indignation flared in her eyes.

'Well, you'd better do it then—else I'll just dump the lot,' he interrupted dismissively.

She narrowed her gaze at him. 'As if you'd be that reckless with an investment.'

'No, you're the reckless one. I'm on damage control. One month.'

Her mouth opened. Then shut. Then opened again. 'You're not going to get *everything* you want.' She sent him another speaking look. 'No more parties.'

'Pardon?'

'While I'm here as your fiancée there'll be no parties.'

Was she trying to dictate terms to him, to renegotiate when she had zero bargaining power? He stifled another laugh. 'I thought you Bohemian types liked parties.'

'Your definition of a party is very different to mine.'

'How so?' He spread his hands in bewilderment. 'I like parties.'

'You like being surrounded by women who pander to your ego.'

He clamped down another smile. She really didn't want other women around, did she? 'No parties at home,' he conceded, happy to be alone with her for what little time he'd have in the house. 'But we dine out. We dance.'

He liked the ambience of a busy restaurant.

'No dancing.'

'Why not?' He folded his arms, amused by her

determined rejection of what he had to offer. 'Don't tell me you can't.'

'Of course I can't,' she declared in total irritation. 'I have no interest in it.'

'I'll teach you,' he said, unbothered. 'Next item?'

'No…' She hesitated. 'No…'

Yes, this was where she really was most vulnerable. 'You don't need to worry.' Hadn't he just told her he only dated one woman at a time?

'I'm not having two fiancés leave me for another woman,' she blurted it out anyway. 'I'm not going through that again. Not even pretend.'

So she had been hurt by the ex-fiancé.

'Fine. You'll break my heart. Unable to get over my rampantly lusty past even though I'll have been nothing but true to you.' He offered the solution softly, watching her closely.

'As if anyone would believe you had.' She rolled her eyes. 'You'll have plenty of women offering to soothe your hurts.'

She was painfully insecure, and breathtakingly insulting, but he didn't blame her. She'd been hurt. 'And you'll have your pride restored.'

A slightly stunned look crossed her face. 'It's not pride.'

'What is it then?'

She shook her head, that expression shutting down. 'You wouldn't understand. You don't seem to have the same kinds of emotions as I do.'

Her words were barbed, and they hit a spot he hadn't realised was exposed. He had emotions all right. It was just that he worked hard to control them. He *had* to. Suddenly raw, he turned and walked towards the door. 'I have to get to work. Be ready for dinner at seven.'

'I don't have any decent clothes with me,' she called after him sulkily.

Drawing in a calming breath, he turned back to face her. 'So buy some more.'

'In case you hadn't noticed, my family has hit the skids. You want to be ashamed by your fiancée when you take her out looking like a bag lady?'

He knew she was deliberately putting obstacles in his way to be as annoying as possible. Too bad, he wasn't going to be bothered. 'You don't look like a bag lady. I like the catsuit thing.' He smiled patronisingly at her. 'But feel free to go out and buy whatever you want for tonight. My treat.'

Her gaze narrowed on his mouth. Awareness arrowed to his groin. He'd known she'd loathe the offer of his money and that her temper would flare. His smile deepened to genuine pleasure in anticipation of her bite.

But she didn't give him a verbal lashing. If anything, she sounded as sultry as a siren. 'What's my budget?'

Only then did she lift her lashes and reveal the fury in her green eyes.

'Will a hundred thousand do to start?' he suggested roughly, unable to resist absorbing her dare and raising the stakes.

She didn't bat an eyelid at that.

He strolled back over to where she still sat on the sofa, enjoying himself immensely. 'We'll have to get you an engagement ring too.' He picked up her hand

and studied her long, delicate fingers. 'Just to really set the whole thing off.'

'That's not necessary,' she clipped, tilting her chin so she could keep burning holes in him with her fiery gaze. 'I'm not wearing a ring.'

So she did have a few scruples. Or maybe she was superstitious.

'You've worn one before.' And he felt a twinge of guilt about pointing that out to her so bluntly.

She tried to pull her hand from his but he gripped it harder.

'And it brought me nothing but trouble,' she muttered.

'Poor Catriona.' He couldn't hold back a second longer. He tugged her hand, drawing her into a standing position, and reached out with his other hand to run his fingers down the length of her beautiful hair. 'Go indulge in some retail therapy,' he suggested with a mercilessly condescending tease. 'Spend hard.'

She sent him another foul look. 'You know I could walk out with all this money of yours and skip the country, never to return.'

'You're too polite to do that. And you know that if you did, I would hunt you down.' His gut clenched at the words. It was only a joke; he didn't mean it. Not truly.

'I'm not afraid of you.'

But he was close enough to have felt her shiver and fought his own primal response to pull her closer and keep her. He wasn't going down that possessive route, not when he knew how destructive it could be. How terrifying. He'd rein this in and get it back to nothing more than a seductive, light tease. 'No, but you're afraid of what I can offer.'

'What do you think that you can offer me that I would be afraid of?'

'The kind of passion you think you can't cope with,' he taunted, leaning that last inch into her space.

'Oh, please.' She rolled her eyes, but he'd seen the rise of that pink under her cheeks.

He put his hands on her slender waist. Satisfaction burst within him, desire for more slammed in on its heels. 'I won't deny I want you in my bed, little Cat,' he muttered, his words tumbling, rough and unstoppable now. 'I'm looking forward to hearing you—'

She suddenly stunned him by clamping her hand over his mouth. 'You think I haven't heard those kinds of sleazy lines before? You want to "pet me until I purr"?' She pushed her hand, forcing him to turn his head away for a second. 'If you really want me, you need to try harder.'

Harder? His laugh was harsh as he pulled her flush against him, pressing his lips on hers. For a spilt-second it was pure passion, lip-to-lip, breast-to-chest, hip-to-hip and straining...but then he made himself go gently again.

Slow. Slow right down.

He'd have his control back, thanks. And he'd surprise her into that deliciously unguarded reaction she'd given him last night.

He softened, pressing small kisses on her plump pouting mouth until she opened it with the smallest of sighs. She tasted like fruit and pastry, a little tart, a lot sweet. And hot. So damn hot and vital. She might be slender, but she was strong. He slid his hand up her back, pressing her closer, needing to feel her where he was aching most. Her hands skated up his chest, curling around his shoulders as she arched her back and her neck, pressing her breasts more firmly against him, letting him deepen the kiss even more. And, heaven knew, he did. Slowly and thoroughly, he explored her mouth, caressing her with his tongue because he couldn't get enough of her taste. He widened his stance so he could gather her closer, aching to absorb all her passion. Gentle was all but forgotten. She felt so good pressed up against him.

And, as she kissed him back, his control started to slip again. He wanted more. He wanted it now.

When she breathed so quickly? When she moaned? When her lips were soft and submissive and hungrily seeking, all at the same time? When her hips circled against his in that way that maddened him to the point of *grinding*?

He teetered on the brink of tumbling her to the sofa, tearing clothing and taking her in a frenzy of unfettered, uncontrolled lust—

He pulled back quickly, resisting the urge. It hurt. His breathing sounded loud in his ears.

But so did hers. To his relief—and pleasure—she still felt warm and soft in his arms. Willing. Ready. So close to *his*. Oh, yes, she wanted him too.

Well, she was going to get what they both wanted. When she was ready. When she asked. And when he was in control. He'd keep it light. Always.

Lit up with amusement and arousal and burning-hot satisfaction, he eyed her lazily. 'I don't think I need to try that hard at all.'

CHAPTER FIVE

'SEXUAL ATTRACTION IS easy enough to ignore,' Kitty argued breathlessly, basically hauling herself upright to stop herself leaning on him.

The man packed a serious sexual punch and she'd succumbed again *so* easily. How on earth did she think she could simply ignore the effect he had on her?

'But why would you want to?' He looked mystified.

She pushed out of his arms and walked away from him, needing the space to clear her head. But goodness, her legs felt wobbly. 'You really are bored, aren't you?'

This was just so easy to him—as natural as breathing. But her heart ached for that something *more*. Surely there had to be more?

'And you really are suffering from a lack of self-esteem.'

She shook her head. 'Don't try to flatter me.'

'I'm being honest. Come on.' He flicked his fingers at her. 'Get ready. I've got to go to work and now we have an errand to run first.'

She stiffened. He was used to calling the shots, wasn't he? 'Then fetch my bag from the communal garden, will you?'

'You stashed your bag in the garden?' He sent her an astounded look, ignoring her attempt at a commanding tone to match his. 'You really are a cat burglar.'

'Bet you can't find it.' She smiled at him coyly.

He sent her another look—a lowering one. 'I know what you're doing.' But he left the room anyway.

Amused, Kitty crossed the library, opened the window and leaned out of it to watch him. He glanced back up to the building, somehow knowing she'd do exactly that. She could feel the heat of his glare across the distance, but then he turned his back on her to study the garden for a few minutes and unerringly went to the bush where she'd hidden the bag.

At that point Kitty flounced away from the window.

A few moments later he returned, triumphantly brandishing her bag. 'You don't have much with you.'

'Because I wasn't planning on staying long.' She snatched it from him and stalked from the room.

'You won't need much anyway...' His sensual laughter followed her down the hall.

Kitty locked the bathroom door and showered quickly, briskly soaping herself and ignoring her hyper-sensitised skin and still trembling legs. She was *crazy* to have accepted this arrangement when he could make her want him so easily.

But chemistry *could* be ignored. And a week or so spent here was a chance to say goodbye to her home. A chance to keep her head high the next time she saw those society wenches. And a chance to prove Alejandro wrong—he wasn't going to get everything he wanted. He wasn't going to get her.

As long as she kept her distance from him. No more touching. No more kissing.

She'd been truly hurt by the end of her engagement to James, but she doubted that Alejandro could ever understand the concept. He was total Teflon. Indestructible and impervious to any pain—of feeling any deep emotion, for that matter. As far as she could tell, life was all a party to him. It was all about the next affair while wheeling and dealing the rest of the time. Well, he wasn't having an affair with her, no matter how good he kissed. She refused to be yet another easy conquest.

When she emerged refreshed she found he'd showered again too and changed into a suit. It was navy with a crisp white shirt but he wore no tie with it and his hair was damp; he looked so sharp her eyes hurt. Her resolve wavered. Did she really think she could resist? That unholy smile lurked in his eyes as he watched her walk towards him and she straightened. Of course she could resist. She wasn't an *animal*.

A car was idling for them just outside the house, an enormous, luxurious thing with a suit-and-sunglasses-clad giant sitting behind the steering wheel.

'You might get away with this kind of ostentatiousness in New York, but it's really not the done thing in London, you know,' she offered faux helpfully once they were ensconced in the back seat. 'Better to take a taxi next time.'

'I prefer to rely on my own driver, but thanks for the advice anyway,' he replied blandly.

The car stopped outside a beautiful old building and Alejandro insisted she went inside with him. Only the subtly placed logo near the heavy wooden door clued her in—this wasn't the kind of bank that had tellers behind security grilles and queues of impatient people. This was exclusivity and discretion to the max. The private banker didn't bat an eyelid when Alejandro insisted he issue Kitty a card then and there, preloaded with his wads of cash.

'Show off,' Kitty murmured as they returned to the waiting car less than twenty minutes later.

Alejandro smiled, but she sensed his attention was flicking from her; his expression had become serious and distant—he was entering 'work mode'. A few minutes later the car pulled in again.

'Paolo and the car are at your disposal all day. Get yourself whatever you need,' he said as he looked out of the window at his new office premises. 'Be there when I get home.'

'Or?'

At her tone he turned back to face her and she realised she'd been wrong about his slipping attention. In this moment, she was the sole object of his searing focus. Her toes curled in her shoes; she was almost melting on the spot.

'Until tonight, sweet fiancée.' He didn't bother replying to her question; he knew he didn't need to.

For a breathless second she wondered if he might take his part too far and kiss her again. But she'd be ready for him this time, right? She'd resist the temptation to slide into his sensuality.

But he didn't lean closer, he didn't kiss her. He just got out of the car.

And that *wasn't* a kernel of disappointment she was feeling. Alejandro waved her off with such a smug, knowing look in his eye that Kitty didn't wave back.

The infuriating creature seemed to know everything she was thinking.

'Where would you like to go, Miss Parkes-Wilson?' Paolo asked politely.

Right now? The moon.

'Could you just drive for a bit while I decide?' She pressed a hand to her hot cheeks.

She needed to come up with a decent plan for the next few days—Alejandro was too confident, but she didn't blame him, only herself. She needed something to combat his intensity.

She'd had no intention of spending a penny of his money when she'd made such a drama about her clothes, but now she felt like making him pay in some small way for his intolerable arrogance.

Maybe she should buy the most outrageous couture item she could find? Maybe she should go for something totally off the wall and appalling that she'd never normally be seen dead in. Amused at the thought, she asked Paolo to take her to the flagship store of a high end designer. But, once she was inside, she was almost immediately distracted by a simple black number hanging on a polished rack right near the door. She moved to take a closer look, inwardly grimacing when she saw there was no price tag.

'Would you like to try it on, madam?' A soft-spoken, impossibly groomed man stepped forward to offer assistance.

'Um…maybe?' she mumbled doubtfully, feeling like a fraud.

She was so used to her 'work wardrobe' of black on black—three-quarter-length trousers and long-sleeved sweaters—she was going to feel weird in anything else. She might have long limbs, but there was so much else required to carry off clothing like this.

One summer in her mid-teen years she'd been scouted by a modelling agency. Not to model swimwear, of course, given her pallor and lack of curves, but high-end fashion. At the time she'd been pleased to get the attention and for a few blissful days had actually believed someone thought she was pretty. But then she'd seen the completed booking sheet with her name on it:

Freak chic. Angular, androgynous, tall with red hair, pale skin. Freckles.

She'd filled out a bit since then, but there was no denying she was still the 'freak' and there was no 'chic' about it. After that dose of reality she'd covered up and come up with her own year-in-year-out version of starving artist attire.

'I believe it would suit you, madam.'

He was clearly paid to say that, but she let him lead her to the changing room anyway.

She straightened her shoulders and followed his example of confident posture. She'd never be considered conventionally pretty, but maybe she could wear the damn designer dresses anyway. A dress like this would be like armour, hiding the weaknesses—the imperfections—underneath. Protecting her. She was *so* tempted.

'I need some statement pieces,' she confided to the attendant as he waited at the entrance to the spacious private room. 'Some dresses that scream exclusive.'

'If I may suggest, nothing screams exclusive more than subtlety,' he replied with a quiet courtesy that had her believing him. 'You go ahead and try this on and I'll be back with more in a moment.'

Kitty quickly stripped and then stepped into the dress, blinking as she regarded her reflection in the gleaming mirror. The dress was beautifully cut and sat perfectly on her waist, but it didn't reveal vast quantities of skin. Maybe the man was right about subtlety?

'Madam—?'

She opened the door and saw the saviour of a salesman had returned with an armload of other options for her to try. But now he paused and studied her with a critical eye.

'Yes.' He nodded as she stood in front of the mirror and she felt as if he actually meant it. 'Our dresses never date,' he informed her confidently. 'And they never lose their value.'

Didn't they? She could well believe that, given they were beautifully tailored and had that sleek sort of design that was recognised the world over. And if they didn't lose their value, then perhaps, as soon as these few weeks were over, she could auction any dresses she bought and then give the proceeds to charity?

That would *definitely* work. She'd be making Alejandro pay, but for her own benefit—not ultimately. And if she did that, then she could spend every last penny of his ridiculous 'budget' just to serve him right. She turned to the assistant, inspired and more enthusiastic about shopping than she'd ever been in her life. 'Then let's see what else you have.'

Somehow four hours flew past. After the dress purchases, she succumbed to the temptation of some

lacy lingerie. Sure, she couldn't exactly auction those
pieces, but the dresses needed the right level of support and discretion—no visible panty lines or bra
straps. It wasn't as if there was any chance of Alejandro seeing her in the lacy smalls…

And then there were shoes—but she chose only a
couple of pairs to see her through.

Lastly she ducked into a beauty parlour and spent a
little of her own money on a spot of personal groom-
ing. Again, if she was going to look the part, she
needed to feel it.

Six and a half hours later she got Paolo to return
her to Parkes House, guiltily figuring she'd better
get on with her actual 'job'. To be honest, she didn't
quite know where to begin. There were so very many
boxes, frankly she wouldn't blame Alejandro at all if
he decided to just send the lot to the rubbish dump.
But she had to start somewhere—and she had to get
it *done*.

'You've been busy,' Alejandro called as he stopped
by the door of the box-filled room two hours later.

Kitty glared at him from where she stood drown-
ing in boxes, overwhelmed by the enormity of all the
stuff she had to process. She'd made the mistake of
opening too many too soon.

Alejandro's mouth twitched, as if he was suppress-
ing a laugh at her expense. 'Did you have fun shopping?'

'Oh, yes, I spent all your money,' she lied, turning
on a brilliant, totally fake smile.

'Well done.' He nodded approvingly. 'I bet that
took some doing.'

She sighed and examined her fingernails in mock

boredom. 'Not really—a handful of dresses, a few pairs of shoes…' she shrugged '…and poof, all the money was gone.'

'Wonderful. You can leave the receipts on the desk in the library for me.' He leaned against the door-jamb and frowned at her black trousers. 'Yet you're not ready to go out?'

'We're going out?' She glanced at the mass of boxes blocking her escape from the room. Her nerves prickled. She was going to have to wear one of those dresses now. She was going to have to live up to the pretence. And she was going to have to look at him across the table… He was too handsome. Too assured. Too damn knowing.

She'd be better off buried in the boxes here.

'Are you not hungry?' Alejandro was feeling ex-tremely hungry and not just for food. She looked beautiful standing there glaring back at him with a raft of emotions flickering across her striking fea-tures. 'I believe it's a good restaurant.'

And they needed to get there soon, before he threw all caution to the wind and tried to seduce her here and now.

'Don't you ever just eat at home?' Her glare be-came less defensive and more curious.

'Why would I?' He didn't enjoy cooking for him-self. Usually he went straight to a restaurant from the office. 'I enjoy socialising with lots of people.'

'Oh.' She nodded and seemed to think about it for a moment. 'So you're aware of how boring your own company is.'

He was stunned into silence briefly, but then laughed grudgingly. 'You witch.'

Her smile of acknowledgement lit up her whole face and made him want to step nearer and feel the warmth of it on his skin. But at the same time he felt compelled to get a dig in.

'So you stay home and cook something gourmet for yourself every night?' he challenged her.

Her smile actually deepened. 'I cook instant noodles every night.'

He grimaced and didn't bother commenting.

'I add fresh vegetables,' she added piously.

'As if that makes it any better.'

'I'm a starving artist,' she said loftily. 'What did you expect me to eat?'

'Well, tonight you can eat like a queen. If you'll only hurry up and get ready,' he groaned.

'Okay, darling, I won't be long.'

He watched her navigate the cardboard obstacles with an impressively swift glide, and walk past him and out of the room with a small toss of her head. Shaking his own, he walked down to the library, pulling his phone from his pocket to check on any mail that might have arrived in the thirty minutes since he'd left the office. He might as well do some more work while he waited. But, to his surprise, it was less than fifteen minutes before she cleared her throat.

He looked up to the doorway and promptly forgot his own name, let alone what it was he'd been writing. 'You can spend every last cent of mine if you're going to end up looking like that.'

Her death stare felled him.

'I'm sensing a colour theme.' He noted the black. Again. He'd not seen her in anything else so far. Black clothes that clung, but covered up almost all of her pale, pale skin. *His* skin tightened. He was looking forward to finally getting a proper glimpse of her.

'I'm grieving the loss of my freedom,' she drawled. 'Hence the mourning outfits.'

He laughed appreciatively. 'It's so hard for you, isn't it? Losing the family home.'

'The long goodbye to the family fine china,' she mused. 'It is a burden.'

'Poor baby, the silver spoon's been snatched from you.'

He wasn't going to make it to the damn restaurant if she kept looking at him like that. He was used to dating very beautiful, perfectly proportioned women, but he'd found none as attractive as he found Catriona right now, with her angular defiance and glittering eyes and her chin jutting in the air. He laughed, more to expend some of the energy coiling inside him than from genuine amusement.

In some ways, his reaction to her wasn't funny at all. He'd been so looking forward to seeing what she had in store for him that he'd actually left work a fraction early because he couldn't wait any longer to find out. It was the first time he'd ever done that for a woman. He'd wanted to check she was still there. Catriona Parkes-Wilson wasn't quite as predictable as all that. But, given he'd instructed Paolo to keep his eye on her, he knew she hadn't left the house again since returning from the epic shopping spree. He also knew exactly how much she'd spent and had to admit it had surprised him. But nothing about Catriona was quite as it seemed and he was interested to see how she was going to play this out.

'Shall we go?'

'Where are we going?' she asked.

He named a new restaurant that—according to his PA—had a waiting list of months.

'There'll be celebrities there.' She frowned and glanced down at her dress.

'Are you going to ask for their autographs?'

A giggle burbled out of her.

'You look amazing,' he assured her briefly. 'We need to leave. Now.'

Now or never. Fortunately, Paolo was waiting with the engine running.

'You can't drive yourself anywhere?' she asked pointedly as he held the door for her.

'Why would I when I can hold hands with you in the back seat instead?' he answered, sliding in after her.

He picked up her hand and felt her curl it into a fist. His sensual awareness was stronger now he knew how good she felt pressed against him. Hell, he wanted that again. Now. The energy between them crackled in the air in the confined space. It took all his willpower not to pull her right into his arms and kiss her into saying yes. Instead, he made himself stay a safe distance away. He could stay in control of this. He would always stay in control.

'Sorry we're late,' he said smoothly as he led her to the two vacant seats his colleagues had left in the middle of the large table at the rear of the restaurant. 'I hope you've gone ahead and ordered.'

Catriona's hand tightened on his. 'You promised no parties,' she whispered as she sat in the seat next to him.

'This isn't a party. This is dinner.' He released her to hold her chair out for her.

'It's a dinner party,' she whispered, pausing. 'There are like...' she glanced around the table '...*fifteen* people here.'

Wasn't that the point of dinner? To socialise? He liked being around people, but she didn't seem comfortable. He took a closer look at her face. 'You okay?'

'I'll just fake it till I make it,' she muttered as she glanced again at everyone at the table before sitting down.

He wasn't even sure he was supposed to hear that little quip, but the honesty underlying it smote him. A small surge of protectiveness made him reach out to clasp her hand in his again as they sat side by side. Did she honestly doubt how stunning she was? Was she really intimidated by these others present?

Or was it that she'd wanted to dine alone with him tonight? His pulse struck an irregular beat. He couldn't remember when he'd last dined alone with a woman. Always he had extras with him—work colleagues and acquaintances, or another couple of women, friends of his latest lover. He liked being surrounded by busy, happy people. That was normal, right? And there was safety in numbers.

Too much time alone with a lover might lead to complications he didn't want.

All he really wanted from the women he dated was physical release and fulfilment—the delights of mutual pleasure. If he took a woman home, he encouraged her to leave after they'd had sex. Generally he'd drive her home, then would drive alone for a while, enjoying the late night and the city, the relaxed state of his body. Or if his lover was fast asleep in his bed—as some of them pretended to be—he went into his study and worked through till dawn. When a woman woke up and realised he wasn't there, she soon got the message. Even when he dated a woman for a few weeks, he wanted his own room at the end of each night. He needed his intimate space to himself. Always. And—other than amusement—he needed his emotions minimally engaged.

'Order something to eat—you'll feel better.' He opted to tease Catriona into sparking back at him. Humour was always good.

'I'm starting to think you must be an emotional eater.'

He laughed. 'No, I just recognise "hangry" when I see it. You didn't stop for lunch—you must be starving.'

'And you know this because?'

'Paolo reported in to me.'

'Oh, so my every move is being documented and reported back to you?'

'Naturally. My fiancée's welfare is very much my concern.'

She glowered at the menu and he bit back his smile.

'Something wrong?' He waited, knowing she'd find something. She was never going to make this easy for him.

'I'm vegetarian.' Her glance at him now was positively sugary. 'So this whole French *foie gras* and raw steak thing isn't working for me.'

Of course she was. 'Another whim of yours?'

She lowered the menu and turned to correct him. 'I've been vegetarian since I was seven.'

'You just made that choice one day?'

'Pretty much.'

'Your parents agreed?'

'Of course not. So I went on hunger strike until they did.'

He grinned, imagining the stubbornness of a red-headed wilful child. 'How long did that take?'

'Just over a week.'

'That long?' He'd have given in to her much sooner. 'Why don't you wish to eat meat—for slimming or ethical reasons?'

She sent him a withering look. 'You really have to ask?'

'When you feel strongly about something, you go the whole way with it, don't you?'

'All or nothing.' She nodded blithely. 'Otherwise what's the point?'

'So when you're wrong, you're *really* wrong.'

'No,' she answered haughtily. 'I'm *rarely* wrong.'

'Oh? What about men?' He laughed, enjoying her cut-glass perfection. 'Third time lucky, do you think?'

'Once I'm shot of you?' she muttered so the others couldn't hear. 'I'm checking in to a nunnery.'

'Oh, no,' he chided. 'That would never do. You'll always need a release for that passion.'

'That's what my art is for,' she said airily.

He laughed, genuinely amused. Catriona had far too much fire for any kind of life of denial.

'What's so funny, you two?' one of the women across the table called to him.

'Alejandro delights in teasing me,' Catriona answered before he could.

He was going to delight in teasing her. Very much.

He listened as she assumed the role of society fiancée. Most of the guests were over from the States like him, a couple of younger ones for the first time, and Catriona efficiently schooled them in the 'off the beaten track' tourist ideas, getting in a plug for her brother's upcoming play too, he noticed with a wry grin. And, for someone who was 'faking it', she was doing a good job. When the food arrived she quietened, tucking in to the specially ordered vegetarian dish with gusto. All or nothing indeed.

'What are you thinking about?' he asked her gently when he saw the curve of a smile on her mouth.

Her eyebrows shot up. 'Seriously?'

'Yes.' He wanted to know everything that was going on in that head of hers.

'I was thinking how delicious that was.'

'So, despite the initial disappointment of the menu, we've managed to please you?'

'Mm hmmm.' She sat back with a satisfied smile and looked at him.

Her eyes sparkled in the light; her skin was so pale it was almost luminescent. She had such striking colouring and, whether she intended it or not, there was challenge in those emerald eyes. Challenge he could no longer resist.

He pushed his chair back and stood. 'Come with me; there's something you need to see.'

'We're leaving now?' She looked startled and glanced back at the other dinner guests.

'Only for a moment. This way.' He threw a polite smile at the others but firmly took her hand and led her out the back and down the gleaming black corridor. At the very end he paused and turned to face her.

'Why are we here?' She still looked bemused. And beautiful.

'To admire this painting.' He waved a distracted hand at a large modernist painting that was conveniently hung on the wall. 'As an artist, I thought you'd appreciate it.'

'I'm not really that much of an artist. And not the painting kind.' She frowned at the canvas.

'Okay, I brought you here because I wanted to be alone with you.' He wasn't afraid to be honest. He knew she wanted him too. And he wanted her to look at him again, not the stupid painting.

She faced him, that frown replaced by a laughing smile, but it still wasn't enough.

'I thought you liked dinner parties with billions of people,' she teased.

'Shh.' He'd hardly touched her all day and he couldn't resist now. He wanted to taste that smile, to press against the pretty pout of her full lips. He wanted to feel her softness and lithe strength, he wanted to claim her body with his own and see her buck and then break under the pleasure he could push her to—

Her eyes widened as she looked up at him. 'Alejandro—'

He caught her lips with his, groaning as he felt her part for him immediately. Caution and control faded. He tugged her closer, pressing her body against the hard ache of his, wrapping his arms around her waist so he could explore her shape. He couldn't get close enough. He tried to keep it gentle, but the kiss deepened. So did his frustration. He wanted to be alone with her. Warm. Naked. He wanted all the time in the world to explore her—to taste every inch and every secret part of her. But he had to make do with just her mouth. It was good. Too good. And it wasn't enough.

Kitty lost track of time and space and sanity. Never had she been kissed like this. Never had she felt as if she was so close to soaring—so high, so quick. There was only Alejandro, only this warmth, only this surging sense of delight. And need. She wanted to burrow closer, she wanted him to touch her more…there… everywhere. His kisses drugged and ignited desire. Never had she wanted a man like this. The way his tongue teased, the way he nipped the inside of her lip with his teeth, the soothing—then stirring—caress of his lips, the pleasure he promised with every stroke…

She writhed helplessly and recklessly against his firm hold, grinding her hips against his. Her wantonness shocked her. She didn't want this to stop. She didn't want this ever to stop. But—oh, God—that was why it had to. They couldn't. Not here. Not now.

She tore her lips from his, jerking her head back and reminding herself of where they were.

'Alejandro,' she pleaded breathlessly, pushing against his chest. 'There are people.'

They were making out in the restaurant corridor like teen lovers who couldn't go home to their parents' houses for privacy, and she felt out of control.

'We're engaged,' he lifted his head and pointed out with annoying reasonableness. 'Of course we're going to kiss. No one would ever believe I was engaged and not be touching my fiancée any time I could.'

She pushed back a strand of hair and sent him a baleful look, locking her knees to stop her legs from shaking. How could he remain so collected when he kissed like that? 'There's an occasional kiss, and then there's indecent behaviour. I only agreed to this so I *wouldn't* get arrested, remember?'

He looked amused. 'A few kisses aren't going to get you arrested. Or were you about to strip naked and have your way with me up against the wall?'

Oh, if he only knew. She jabbed her finger in his chest. 'Stop provoking me.'

'But it's the most fun I've had in years.' He pulled her close again and brushed another quick kiss on her lips. 'You respond so magnificently. Like lightning, you flare. You must be incandescent when you orgasm.'

A wave of heat almost turned her to cinders on the spot. 'Right now I'm incandescent with rage.' She wished the lighting in the corridor was dimmer so he couldn't see how violently he was making her blush. 'Stop talking like that.'

He bent his head and whispered in her ear, 'But it's turning you on.'

'Everyone is staring,' she hissed. Well, only the couple of people who'd ventured down the corridor, and they'd quickly gone again.

'I don't care.'

'Well, *I* do.' She pushed hard against his chest. If he kept kissing her like that she'd agree to anything he suggested and she refused to let him win so easily. 'It's past my bedtime.'

'You want to go home to bed?' He stepped back and looked wickedly at her.

'Alone,' she lied. 'Yes.'

'Then let's get you there.'

CHAPTER SIX

OFFICIALLY, PARKES HOUSE had eight bedrooms, all of them with private bathrooms. Half were on the second floor, the remainder on the third.

'Which room did you take?' Alejandro asked as they climbed the stairs. 'The one next to mine?'

'Of course not.' It had interested her to see that he'd claimed one of the smaller rooms as his, but maybe that was just because there was so much stuff shoved into all the others.

'So you know which is mine.' He grinned. 'Did you go in and take a good look at my things?'

'Naturally.' She battled her blush and tried to act as if she wasn't embarrassed. 'The more one knows about one's enemy, the better one is equipped to win the battle.'

'Enemy?' He laughed. 'Bit extreme, don't you think?' He took hold of her hand. 'Did you learn anything of use?'

She gently breathed out, trying to slow her pounding pulse. 'You're a show-off. As if you can read all those books at once.' The pile beside his bed had almost exclusively been non-fiction, on a wide and eclectic range of subjects.

'I like reading,' he said. 'You won't find the diamonds, by the way. I keep them with me at all times. They're too precious.' He looked at her curiously as they walked along the corridor of the third floor. 'So which room?'

Her heart still thudded too quickly. She had no idea how she was going to resist him. 'My own.'

His eyes glinted. 'And it's not one of these?' They'd passed all the doors now.

She shook her head.

'Show me.'

'Fine.' She led him to the stairwell again and went first.

'You were up in the attic? Servants' quarters?'

'Don't go thinking I was some kind of Cinderella,' she said gruffly. 'In some ways I was very spoilt.'

'Tell me something I don't know,' he drawled.

She glanced at him but he was smiling. At the top she went a few paces along the much narrower corridor, opened the door, flicked on the light switch and then stood back to let him go in first.

'Oh…' He muttered something under his breath.

'What?' She peeked around the doorway, stopping when she saw he'd halted only a few steps into the room.

He turned to face her. 'It's so light.'

She glanced at the white walls, white furnishings and the myriad small windows that gave the most glorious views to the skies. She couldn't help smiling because he was right—the light was what made this room. Even at night, it had a brilliant quality. She couldn't believe he'd not seen it before.

'Have you not been up here at all?' She was amazed

as he shook his head. 'You bought this house and everything in it without even taking a proper look?'

'I liked the location, the convenience to work and the outlook.' He shrugged. 'Anything else I want I can add or rebuild later.'

Didn't he see what was special about the place—its history, its quirks, its sense of *home*?

'I liked the view up here. The light and the space.' She tried to explain it to him as she walked past him. The angles of the ceiling were random because of the roofline. When she'd turned thirteen she'd had the room enlarged to become both her bedroom and her first sculpture studio. Her father hadn't minded paying for the renovation and it had kept her occupied and away from the parade of women he was bringing home. She'd been unable to compete with those beauties who'd turned his attention from his children. She'd spent hours alone up here.

Alejandro was staring grimly at the narrow single bed in the corner with its plain white coverings. Then he turned those penetrating eyes on her. 'Did you sneak boys up here to share this bed?'

'Of course not. What kind of a question is that?' She stuck her hands on her hips and shook her head at him. 'You have such a one-track mind.'

He laughed at her reaction and her heart started its crazy trip-along pace again. 'Oh, come on, all those times using that secret hidden key of yours?' He folded his arms and leaned against the wall, looking utterly roguish.

'Absolutely not.'

Sneaking a lover in was totally the sort of thing

he'd have done. No doubt he'd been sowing his wild oats since he was a youth.

'I was a good girl,' she added when he kept staring at her with those dangerous eyes.

'You amaze me,' he said dryly. 'Then why the need to sneak in and out if it wasn't to go wild?'

'I was exploring the art scene.' And pushing boundaries to get her father's attention. It hadn't worked.

'So you were the young muse for the Bohemian set?' He waggled his brows at her.

'Actually, my first boyfriend was three months *younger* than me. He was another art student when I was at *university*.'

'Was it sublime?'

Of course it wasn't. She turned her back on his low laughter.

'Poor Catriona. And then there was the dastardly fiancé.'

She hated that he guessed her lack of experience so easily. 'It's not that easy for everyone, you know,' she muttered grimly.

It was a disappointment. She would have liked to have been one of those free spirits who flitted from romance to romance and emerged unscathed, but it wasn't to be. She was nothing like Alejandro. And she didn't want to be with someone who she knew would let her down. Sure, she had his attention now— for whatever reason—but soon enough that attention would turn to someone else and she'd be left in the cold again.

His hands on her shoulders pulled, turning her to face him. 'I'd make it sublime.'

His smile was bewitching, but it was something in his eyes that really had her spellbound.

'You're full of promises,' she muttered gruffly, trying to settle her skipping pulse.

'Ah, so you want proof.'

She didn't know what she wanted any more. But she knew this moment had been building since they'd first set eyes on each other. It was normal for him but so outside her realm of experience she didn't know how to handle it.

'Do you always get what you want?' she asked, genuinely curious.

'When I've decided I want something, I stop at nothing until I have it,' he said, equally honest. Equally serious. 'So, yes, I do.'

'And right now you want me?'

He nodded.

'And you'll stop at nothing?'

He didn't answer. A smile, slow and amused, spread over his face. He tugged her that little bit closer and bent his head to kiss her. And she didn't say no. She didn't step back. She just let him. She stood there and let him pull her into his hot embrace.

And she liked it.

She moaned as he moved her that bit closer, his kiss claiming her. Soft kisses again, teasing ones, tender and tormenting. She pressed closer, seeking more. His hand swept down her back, resting on her hip. It was no longer enough. None of this was enough.

Her legs were shaking. She couldn't stand it any more. Literally couldn't stand.

But she didn't need to say anything. His arms had already tightened about her and somehow the bed was now at the back of her legs. With a smooth movement he eased her onto the narrow little mattress and then came down on top of her. She gasped, trembling at the sensation of finally having him there, so close to her.

He muttered something but she didn't catch it because he'd resumed stroking, trailing those torturously slow fingertips across her waist and up to cup her breast. Her body ached. She longed to burst free of her clothes, even her skin. She was *so* hot. He looked into her eyes for a wordless moment. Passion had darkened his eyes even more and she just drowned in them. His skin was slightly flushed. She didn't think she'd ever seen him look as gorgeous—or as dangerous. Every cell within her tightened in anticipation.

He smiled and she was lost. His hand framed her face, fingers tangling in her hair, and he kept her still so he could savour her lips, plundering her mouth with his tongue. Teasing, touching, until the yearning inside could no longer be contained. Then it wasn't as teasing, wasn't as gentle. Hunger sharpened.

He couldn't seem to get enough of kissing her. Which was good, because she couldn't get enough of kissing him. She arched, aching to get nearer, wanting him everywhere, in every way. Her legs splayed, allowing him the space to press closer, more intimately against her. She groaned as his hard length pressed against her, right there. So good. Uncontrollably she rocked, rubbing against him, trying to ease the need, skating closer and closer to an arousal that could have only one end. Her bra was too tight, her breasts were too full, her nipples too taut. Finally, finally, blessedly, he moved, kissing down the length of her neck until his hot mouth hit the high line of her dress.

She clenched on her muscles and cried out as need spiked within her as he pressed his open mouth against her jutting nipple, through the fabric and all. He stiffened above her then swiftly returned to kiss her full on the mouth. Not tender at all now, but ravenous. She couldn't contain another moan of desire, couldn't stop the ragged, short breaths of desire escaping her lips.

'I want to see you,' he muttered savagely.

His hands dropped to her thighs, to the hem of her dress.

'I want to see every inch of you.'

Kitty opened her eyes, his passion-roughened words shocking her back to reality. The light hurt. It was so light in here. She didn't want to be seen by him in this unforgiving brightness. She didn't want him to see all her imperfections. In that split second she couldn't help comparing herself to all the other women he'd known—all those beautiful women. She gripped his hand, stopping him from lifting her dress any higher. There were very, very few people who'd seen her naked. And it would never happen in this bright light. Not with him, not with anyone.

Her emotions spiralled out of control as she realised where she was and what she was doing and with whom and *what was she thinking?* This behaviour was so unlike her. Never had she wanted a man the way she wanted him. It shocked her. It almost scared her.

She froze.

He raised his head and looked down at her, his gaze both astute and tense, his smile rueful. 'You're not ready to let me in, Catriona?'

Dazed, she looked up into his face from where she lay half beneath him. For a fatalistic moment she thought she would *never* be ready to cope with him.

His smile deepened—a little strained, a little tender. 'I think you need to sleep on it.' He levered off the bed.

'You're…leaving?' Even though he was no longer pinning her, she couldn't move, she was stunned. And suddenly desolate.

'Perhaps I have more patience than you give me credit for.' He braced his arms either side of her, leaning over her again only to press a quick, light kiss on her lips. 'I will never do anything you don't absolutely want me to. Let's be very clear on that.'

He straightened and walked away from her before she could think what to say. Kitty sat up, watching him as he left the room. She was hot and cold and confused and part of her was relieved but the other part was nothing short of devastated. As soon as he'd closed the door behind him, she slumped back onto the bed—suddenly sorry that he'd been so restrained. She could have had an experience unlike any other if she'd not been so self-conscious. So insecure. So stupid.

If he'd kissed her for just a few minutes more she'd have been so het-up she'd have agreed to anything. But he wasn't going to let it happen that way. He was too sensitive to her moods. He wanted her commitment to their affair to be made beforehand—not in the heat of the moment. It turned out he was too damn chivalrous to make it easy for her.

She rolled onto her stomach and buried her face in her pillow in a swelter of confusion and desire and contradiction. It was only lust, right? She could get a grip on herself—it shouldn't be that difficult. But the thing was, she did want him and he knew it. He was just going to make her say it so there was no doubt.

Could she take the little he offered? Was it even that little? She'd never had that kind of an affair. Never had the kind of pleasure he'd already made her feel in just those few touches. Maybe she *could* handle it. And maybe, once it was done, it would be over. The desire would die because this driving need would have been filled. All she had to do was swallow her pride and say yes to him.

But she couldn't bring herself to do that either. She didn't want this to be that easy for him. She didn't want to be just another of his notches.

Basically? She was screwed.

She gave up on sleep and rose super early the next morning and grumpily trooped downstairs to the kitchen to find some fruit to freshen her up. But she encountered Alejandro on the second floor landing in shorts and a thin tee, looking hot and sweaty and, when he caught sight of her, grumpy. He'd clearly been out for a run or something. So that was how he did it.

'How I do what?' he asked.

She choked—had she uttered that thought aloud? She must have; he was gazing at her expectantly. But he still wasn't smiling.

Awkwardly, she tried to explain. 'Eat all that rich food but stay so...'

'What?' he prompted when she broke off.

'Fit,' she mumbled.

He didn't smile. If anything, his expression grew

even grimmer. 'Is that what you wear to bed?' He gestured at her white pyjamas. 'You wear black during the day and white at night. That's very you.'

They stared at each other across the landing and for a moment neither moved.

'Please be ready to go out when I get home tonight,' he said gruffly. 'Unlike some, I work a long day and when I'm done, I'm hungry.'

Her spine stiffened. 'Certainly, darling. I won't make you wait a second longer than necessary.'

Her gaze clashed with his.

'God,' he muttered hoarsely, 'I hope not.'

Alejandro threw himself into work, determined to put Catriona out of his mind for the day and concentrate on everything else. But thoughts of her eroded his focus. He'd never met a woman like her—intriguing, contrary. Annoying. She made him laugh. And the feeling of her strong yet soft body arching to meet his? The sound of her breathy moans as her desire escalated?

He puffed out a long-held breath and turned away from his computer in disgust. He was getting nowhere. He fished in his pocket, then laid the diamond choker across the desk. He wanted to see her wearing it again. He wanted to see her wearing the diamonds and nothing else. But that was what had shut her down last night—when he'd said he wanted to see her, she'd stiffened in his arms. She had an insecurity there that he was going to have to sweep clear somehow.

He deliberately worked late because he wanted to prove to himself that he could stay away from her. That he was still in control of himself emotionally and physically. This was nothing, this was easy, this was still *safe*. But when he finally headed home, his pulse started pounding. It was all he could do not to bolt up the stairs and haul her into his arms.

He didn't bolt. He just walked. Still in control.

But his pulse sprinted.

He found her in one of the box-filled upstairs bedrooms. She was in black again—long-sleeved top, slimline trousers and thin black sneakers on her feet. Her hair hung loose down her back, as glorious as ever. His blood fizzed. Just seeing her was a pleasure, but her mouth was downturned as she bent over another enormous cardboard box. She had a clipboard beside her, ready to itemise everything she extracted.

He glanced about the room. He had little sentimentality, but maybe the loss of these things truly made her sad.

'What are these?' He nudged the box she'd been looking into.

'Oh.' She glanced up, startled, and coloured slightly. 'They're the Christmas and birthday presents I gave my father every year since I was about eight. My earliest sculptures. He obviously didn't feel the need to keep them.'

She shrugged.

Alejandro knew there were issues with her father. He'd found him to be somewhat unreliable in his business practice—the amount left behind in the house had been totally downplayed, for one thing, and it seemed Catriona and her father were not close. But Alejandro knew some fathers were worse than others. His father was the worst of all.

Distracting himself, he lifted some of the pottery

pieces out. Some had not stood the test of time. Or at least hadn't been kept in a safe place. There were chipped bits and a couple of broken vase tips at the bottom of the box. But a couple—especially one vase and a sculpture that looked like a lion—were very delicate and showed the development of skill. 'Some are—'

'Terrible, I know.' She interrupted him with a brittle laugh. 'I was just a kid. He didn't think I should study art; apparently I needed to get a real job. You know, the kind that earns money. Because that was what mattered most to Dad. The guy who'd married into an old wealthy family and managed to *lose* all the money...' She trailed off and glanced at Alejandro with a wistful smile. 'Your parents must be very proud of you.'

It felt as if a boulder had been lodged in his chest. For a second he gaped before collecting himself. She didn't know about his parents then. She didn't know...

He halted his thoughts. He didn't feel inclined to tell her. He never discussed it and ensured conversation never became personal enough for a woman to ask. Several business colleagues knew, but also knew never to mention it. He turned away from the box. 'Are you ready for dinner?' he asked bluntly.

'Time sneaked away from me.' Kitty bit her lip, surprised to see icy reserve sweep over him. 'I only need five minutes if we're going out again?'

He'd totally stiffened up, no longer the suave conversationalist and tease.

'Of course.'

She sent him a cautious smile and left the room, quickly moving to change her clothes. Why had he frozen up when she'd referenced his family? It was unlike him to reveal so much; usually he teased to deflect a conversation. A million more questions followed—where did that slight exotic edge to his accent come from? Why was he so driven when he'd had so much success so young? He fascinated her and she wanted to know everything about him.

But at dinner she found that goal impossible to reach. The guests chatted animatedly about topical issues but no one pressed her for any detail about her relationship with Alejandro, no one asked how they'd met or when they'd become engaged. Which was polite. But no one asked him anything intrusive or illuminating either, which was disappointing. They sought his opinion on something to do with work, or debated politics and current affairs. It was all intelligent and interesting, but the only other thing she learned about him was that he was well read, had encyclopaedic general knowledge and would be an extremely useful addition on a pub quiz team.

And as the evening progressed she realised he didn't actually talk that much at all. He smiled and gave a thoughtful insight into something that was business-related or added an occasional witty comment, but, for the most part, his contributions were limited. He seemed happy just to be at the centre of the noise and chatter. Her curiosity deepened.

But she knew she wasn't the only curious one at the table. The woman sitting opposite her had been avidly watching Alejandro, conversing with him loudly, unsubtle in trying to get his attention. Now she turned to Kitty—her curiosity unveiled as she raked her gaze over her, her eyes narrowing on Kitty's hand.

'Still no ring?' The woman's smile gleamed as she leaned across and spoke in an undertone. 'There's a smidge of hope for the rest of us then.'

The last thing Kitty wanted was to compete for Alejandro—not in any way.

'You're welcome to have him,' she replied directly, but with a smile. 'I keep trying to shake him off, but he's persistent.'

There was a moment of stunned silence around the table. Kitty swallowed; she hadn't realised she'd spoken *that* loudly.

'After Catriona's hurt over her previous engagement, she's decided an engagement ring is bad luck,' Alejandro said with urbane ease. 'I have agreed to surprise her on our wedding day when our vows are taken.' He placed his hand over hers and gave it a squeeze. 'She finds it difficult to trust, but I'm working on it.'

Kitty stared at him, unable to think of a thing to say to that. He met her eyes for a moment, and she saw the humour dancing in his, but there was something else too. Something she couldn't define and couldn't cope with. She turned and caught a stabbing glance at her from the other woman, but she was too floored by Alejandro to bother responding. Her body felt engulfed in flames. She was so embarrassed, but also somehow grateful. It was crazy. She was crazy. And so was he.

'You're a more outrageous liar than I am,' she whispered in his ear in the most provocative way she could manage once normal conversation had resumed, determined to take control of this mad roller coaster ride again. 'That was pretty good. But you know, I've changed my mind. I want a rock. Monstrous huge, please. The gaudiest thing you can drop a few hundred thousand on.'

She sat back and beamed at him.

He cupped her face and inexorably drew her close again so he could whisper in return, 'It's too late; the offer is rescinded. I like my story better about the bad luck engagement ring. It has an air of truth about it.'

He was so near she was lost in the depth of his black-brown eyes. Her heart raced. He was horrendously handsome. She scrambled to stay sane—to stay on top of what was just a game.

'You're heartless. Utterly heartless.'

He laughed delightedly; his warm breath stirred her hair. For a moment it was as if they were in their own bubble of amusement and heat.

'I have no need for a heart,' he muttered.

That hit like a cold wind. Could anyone really be that carefree? She pulled back, wary of the other diners watching them less than surreptitiously. With an effort she maintained her smile and reached for a glass of water.

'Lead me along as far as you dare, Catriona,' he added quietly so only she heard. 'I'll keep step. You won't scare me off.'

'I thought you were out to stop me from saying outrageous things.'

'I've decided I like them. The only person they really cause trouble for is you.'

And wasn't that the truth.

'I am chastened,' she admitted honestly. 'That's it—no more from me.'

He laughed, full bodied and sexy. 'Never. You're too impulsive for that vow to last long.'

The truth was she was trying as hard as she could to hold him off. Because this sparring—this foreplay—was fun. But once she'd given in to him—and to her own desire—it would be over. It was all in the thrill of the chase for him. He'd be off on the next hunt once he'd captured this prey. So, back at Parkes House, she didn't let him climb the stairs with her.

'No. No. No. No.' She scampered ahead of him and held up her hands like a metaphorical wall. 'You stay down there.'

He looked up at her, pausing with one foot on the first step. His mouth quirked. 'Not even a kiss good-night?'

'No. Nothing. Not a thing.'

He leaned back against the railing and his smile broadened to positively smug. 'Finding it so hard to resist you can't even risk one kiss?' Amusement danced in his eyes. 'Not long now then.'

His arrogant laughter followed her. He was appalling.

And that was the thing, wasn't it? This wasn't ever going to be for long.

CHAPTER SEVEN

'I'M READY.' KITTY looked up as Alejandro walked in from a frustrating day.

His mouth dried. She was sitting on the sofa in the library with her ankles demurely crossed, clad in another slinky black dress that clung to her curves and suggested total sensuality while keeping her too damn covered up.

Was she ready for him?

He'd let her get away without so much as a kiss yesterday but now he'd had enough. This was the longest amount of time he'd ever invested in a seduction and seeing her sitting there so coolly perfect was the last straw. Hadn't she spent the day thinking of him? Wasn't she being eaten from the inside out by coiling desire the way he was?

'Alejandro?' Her eyes widened as she watched him stalk towards her.

He didn't reply as he pulled her up from the sofa and into his arms. This was what he needed. Her close in his arms, her mouth parting under his, her body softening.

He kissed her the way he'd been fantasising about all day. Long and deep and hungry. His arms tightened as he felt her lean into him. Desire raced as she kissed him back, her energy rising to meet his in a snap. Oh, yes. Ready. So ready.

He lifted his head to look into her eyes for the consent he so badly needed. But she pushed him back breathlessly.

'Stop it,' she panted. 'You're messing up my hair. It took hours to get it this smooth, you know.'

'And it looks lovely.' He reached for her again. He needed to do more than look—he needed to touch. Now. 'Come back here.'

'No—' she stepped further away '—I didn't do it for you.'

'No?' He smirked.

'Of course not!' She rolled her eyes. 'It's for all those wannabe lovers of yours. The troupe of women hanging on your every word. I have to show my cred to them.'

Alejandro paused, dropping his hand. That was ridiculous. She had nothing to prove. 'They think you're my fiancée.'

'Like that matters to them!' She faced him. 'Or to you.' She shook her head. 'If one took your fancy, you'd be gone in a flash.'

He frowned, his irritation building. The last thing he felt like doing was leaving her. And suddenly the last thing he felt like was sharing her with a bunch of other people around the dinner table either. He wanted all her attention on *him*. As his was on her.

'Can you even remember all their names?' she asked.

He stared at her, mystified.

'All your ex-lovers,' she explained grumpily.

It was his turn to roll his eyes. 'Can they remember mine? What does it matter?' They were irrelevant to this. 'What's wrong with living in the moment?'

'It's just so…meaningless.'

And? He really didn't see why she wanted complication, for things to be involved. 'Must you be so deep all the damn time? Must there be meaning in everything?'

'Not everything all of the time. But sometimes. Yes.'

'Work hard, play hard. That's the life I enjoy.' And he didn't see why his past should impact on his affair with her now. He didn't understand why she railed against what they could share in bed together. 'I already told you—I will never marry. I will never have children.'

She hesitated, her fire dropping a fraction. 'You don't like them?'

'It is not something that interests me.' He turned away from her pretty eyes.

'Oh, that's a shame. Who's going to inherit all your billions, then?'

He laughed, relieved to hear her tart tone. She was back to her best with him. 'I'm going to give it away to charity.'

'Nice.' She nodded. 'Just the one charity or are you going to share it around, the way you do your sex skills?'

Ouch. He rubbed his chest with the heel of his hand. 'You're not going to try to convince me to have children? Tell me I'd make a great father?'

'If you don't want them, you don't want them. Who am I to try to convince you otherwise?'

'You want children?' Oddly, his chest felt heavier

now. The thought of Catriona cradling a small child made it hard to breathe.

'Possibly.' A wary expression flitted over her features. 'But I'd have to find a decent guy first. In my experience, they're thin on the ground.'

He chuckled, trying to recover his equilibrium. 'Poor princess. You've gone from—how do they say—from the frying pan to the fire.'

'You said it,' she agreed dramatically. 'I escaped the claws of a cad only to fall into the jaws of a shark.'

From one heartbreaking engagement to one fake one. The fake one was more fun, though.

'You'll survive,' he said soothingly. 'You might even have fun.'

Silently, she met his gaze. Her eyes sparkled. She was having fun now and they both knew it.

She drew in a breath and lifted her chin that fraction higher. 'So how many other people are going to be at dinner tonight? Will there be any other men for me to flirt with or will it just be women to fawn over you and stroke your ego?'

Yes, the game was on again. Tension coiled in his muscles at the thought of dinner; he didn't want any distractions now.

'It'll just be the two of us,' he muttered, making that decision then and there. They needed time alone together to get this sorted between them.

'Not the usual entourage?' She turned limpid eyes on him. 'Are you sure you can cope with the depth of conversation that might be required?'

'I think I can keep up with you.'

'So where are we going?' she asked softly.

He didn't know. He quickly texted his assistant to

let him know that he and Catriona were not going to be joining the others for dinner then challenged the beautiful woman still standing too far away from him. 'You're the local; you lead the way.'

She skimmed a sharp gaze over his Armani suit and then looked down at her couture dress. 'I'm not familiar with all those super exclusive restaurants you seem to like.'

He shrugged. 'There'll be something nearby.'

He didn't want it to be too far from his bed. As far as he was concerned, tonight she was going to be his.

They ended up in a small Thai takeaway joint. She leaned against the Formica counter, laughing as she ordered a selection for them both.

'You like it spicy?' She sent him a coy look.

'I can't believe you even have to ask.'

'I don't like it too hot,' she said primly.

'I don't believe you.' He flicked her chin. 'I see through you.'

She turned so she faced the other way to see out of the window and watch the passers-by. 'Maybe I see through you too.'

Did she, now? He leaned closer. 'What do you think you see?'

'Someone who sells himself short.'

His eyebrows shot up. Uh, no, he didn't. He knew what he was good at.

'You have much more to offer than good-looks, money-making brains and superb sex skills.'

Both sassy and serious, she stole his breath.

'Oh?' He didn't want to ask. Didn't want it to matter. But suddenly her opinion had value. 'What else do I offer?'

'Humour.' She reached for the carrier bags from the waiter and then glanced at him. 'And you're kind.'

He stilled on his way out of the tiny restaurant. 'You've clearly mistaken me for someone else.'

'Oh, you can have your cruel moments.' She bit her lip ruefully and led him out onto the pavement. 'But you can't hide your underlying tendency towards kindness. You didn't drop me in it in front of all those people at your party. You're letting me sort my family's stuff even though a professional would be much faster, but you know it matters to me.'

He cleared his throat. 'I think you'll find that *kindness* isn't my motivation.'

Her eyes glinted but she shook her head. 'You're fundamentally okay,' she argued. 'I just don't think you realise it. You look after your staff, you go to great lengths to take care of your guests and you actually *do* give money to charity.' She turned and walked snappily along the path. 'Now, we could sit in the garden if you like. As long as you can handle eating with plastic cutlery?'

'I guess,' he muttered dryly, following a pace behind. But the number of times in his youth when he'd eaten with no cutlery... Hell, the number of meals he'd missed because there was no money even to buy bread. She might think she could manage on a bit of a budget now, but she had no idea of his reality. And she had no real idea of him.

Kind? He didn't feel in the least kind regarding her.

He sprawled back on the lawn, recovering from her direct assessment of him, his appetite lost. But he enjoyed watching her, listening to her chattering about her day, about the city, about anything, prompting her with a question when she fell silent. He needed her to distract him from the desire tightening his muscles.

The warm dusk slowly turned into a cool evening. The last of the sunlight made strands of her hair spark. Her vitality glowed. All he wanted to do was reach out and capture it—capture *her*. Yeah, not kind.

'It was good?' he asked as she helped herself to the last spoonful of his curry.

'Mm hmmm,' she mumbled as she finished the mouthful.

'So you do like it hot,' he muttered triumphantly.

She smiled at him and he was felled.

'Let's go home.' The words spilled out. But the second they left his mouth his innards chilled.

Since when did he think of Parkes House as his *home*? Let alone think of *her* as being part of that? And this desire to capture her and hold her close? He froze as his heart slammed his chest. He tried to block the fear trickling in. Catriona was just another woman he was seducing. That was all.

Just another lover who he could take. Or leave.

CHAPTER EIGHT

KITTY WORKED QUICKLY and efficiently, categorising items before re-boxing them neatly, mortified her father had left such a mess for a total stranger to deal with. Much ought to be taken to the rubbish or recycling centre and the sooner the better because she was totally over the blow-hot, blow-cold enigma that was Alejandro Martinez.

He'd fallen silent on the short walk home last night and then vanished to his room without a word—no goodnight call, let alone goodnight kiss. He'd gone to work without speaking to her this morning as well. Which was *fine* and she was *not* disappointed and she should *not* have spent all day trying to work him out. Except he consumed her thoughts. Why did he sometimes seem so unhappy despite all his success? There were moments when she thought an expression of pure pain crossed his face—it had flashed out of the blue when they'd walked home last night. He'd utterly iced up. She didn't understand why—they hadn't been talking anything personal.

She sighed and taped down another box. The mystery of his life was no business of hers; she just needed to get a grip on her own reaction to him.

She was not up for a roller coaster ride of his engineering.

The slam of the front door echoed all the way up to the room where she was working. She glanced at the clock. It was only four in the afternoon, way too early for him to have finished work already.

'How's it going?' he asked as he appeared in the library doorway the merest moment later, all tense angles in a navy suit, no tie and no smile.

'I hate my father for letting it get to this state,' she admitted honestly, trying not to stare at him, but failing.

Alejandro's edgy expression softened. 'Another day nearer to your precious necklace. You suffer so for your diamonds.'

'Why are you back so early?' She watched him hovering just inside the room. 'Shouldn't you be running your empire?'

'It's running successfully without me for a few hours.' He looked into the nearest box and poked through the contents. 'It's a test for the new employees.'

'Really?'

He looked back to her. 'No,' he said bluntly.

The atmosphere thickened. Her heart thudded too quickly for comfort. She was too acutely aware of that raw look in his eyes that she didn't understand. He looked as if he hadn't slept well.

Don't get curious. Don't think you're starting to care.

She tried to warn herself—her mother had fallen for a suave, charming swine and so had she in James. She didn't need to make that mistake again. She didn't need him coming home all intense and brooding and pulling her close only to then push away without a minute's notice. But an impulse was rising—she wanted to see his smile again. She wanted him to tease again.

Alejandro's gaze dropped and he sombrely studied the contents of the box nearest him.

'I was thinking you're right,' he said slowly.

Kitty's jaw dropped but before she could speak he flashed the quickest of grins.

'That I should understand more about this house,' he added, walking away from her, the smile gone again. 'And I might as well do that while you're here to explain it to me.'

She was wary of the intense energy emanating from him. Of this seemingly random request. What did he *really* want?

'Where did you want to start?' she asked as he restlessly prowled round the room, picking up small items and replacing them haphazardly and seeming to avoid looking at her directly.

He fiddled with a small wooden figurine on the table. 'Show me your favourite things.'

She kept watching him steadily but he still didn't meet her gaze.

'I don't have favourite things as much as I have favourite places,' she said.

'Such as the library?'

She wrinkled her nose. 'I used to wait for my father here and it was always a disappointment. That's why Teddy left notes for me in the hidden compartment in the bookcase—to cheer me up.'

He'd left notes because most of the time Teddy

was out, supposedly at sports coaching when in fact he was at the local drama club.

'So then it's your bedroom?' Alejandro guessed.

'That came later,' she corrected him. 'My favourite place of all is the secret room.'

He spun towards her, his eyebrows high. 'There's a secret room?'

She laughed, pleased at the flash of interest in his face. 'I know—it's pretty cool.'

'It wasn't on the plans.'

'If it was, it wouldn't be secret!' She rolled her eyes. 'Come on—it's downstairs. It's not huge; it's about the size of a lift compartment.'

'And it exists because…?'

'Because it was an extension of the butler's pantry and its entrance got sealed and hidden because one of my ancestors was a scoundrel and needed to hide from the long arm of the law.'

He stared slack-jawed at her. 'Seriously?'

He laughed as she nodded.

'That sounds like one of your family. Good God!' He walked to the door. 'Show me.'

She overtook him on the stairs, unable to stop her small smile at the thought of sharing the house's secret with him. She'd always loved this little room. 'So, through the kitchen and then out to here.'

'Where every kitchen appliance known to man is stored,' he said dryly.

'That's right,' she acknowledged ruefully. Her father had indulged their old chef back in the day before the money had dried up.

She walked into a corner of the pantry and pushed the old subtle knob that formed part of the decorated skirting board. There was a clunking noise and a part of the wall swung, revealing a narrow gap.

'Oh, my—'

'I know.' She interrupted him. 'Hardly anyone knows it's here.' She squeezed in the gap, her own excitement at being back in the small room rising. 'It's really cute.' She glanced into the far corner where, as a girl, she'd set up a cosy hiding place. Slowly she turned, suddenly remembering. 'But, whatever you do, don't—'

She broke off as he shut the door behind him.

'Don't what?' he asked.

The darkness was complete.

'Oh,' he said, quick to realise. 'We'll have to feel for the door handle?'

'Actually, there's a slight design flaw,' she mumbled in embarrassment. 'No lighting. No interior door handle.'

'Why am I not surprised?' he sighed. 'Are we going to suffocate to death?'

'No, there's a vent.'

'Thank heavens for small mercies. Do I need to break the door open?'

'No, don't damage it,' she said quickly. That old mechanism was too historic and she'd hate its secret to be exposed. 'Can't you call one of your assistants to come and direct them how to open it?'

'I don't have my phone with me.'

Oh. 'I don't either,' she realised. She'd left it on the table upstairs. 'We're stuck.'

Heat flooded her at the realisation. She was locked in, alone and in the dark, with one very sexually magnetic man who was the walking definition of unpredictable.

'There's really no way of opening it from this side?' he asked, a thin vein of irritation in his voice.

'No.' She'd tried hard enough as a girl.

He was silent for a moment and she heard him stepping around, getting the feel for the space. 'Paolo should be here in an hour or so to drive us to dinner. He'll come in through the kitchen entrance; will we hear him arrive?'

'Yes.'

'And will he be able to hear us if we yell?'

'Yes.' She'd yelled when she was a child a few times.

'Then...' He paused. 'I guess we wait.'

For an hour or so. She leaned against the back wall and slid down into her old familiar corner, blocking her mind from sending her images of what they could do to pass the time. She was *not* going to be that easy for Alejandro.

'You know this is dangerous,' he said a bit roughly. 'How did you get out of here when you were a kid?'

She cleared her throat. 'I taped a ribbon over the edge so the door couldn't quite lock into place, but it was almost shut so no one knew I was here.' Or at least that's what she'd pretended. The chef had always known and had always checked on her. Neither of her parents had.

'What did you do in here all by yourself?'

'Drew. Dreamed.' She'd sat with her torch and sketched fanciful creatures—fairies goblins, elves. She smiled self-consciously at the memory—which was stupid, given he couldn't see her. But it was that kind of place for her—secret and a little bit magic.

'You couldn't do that upstairs?'

'When Mother was at home, my father stayed out very late.' Her smile faded. She'd sat in the library and waited for him. 'And when she was away he brought a lot of "guests" home. I preferred to stay out of their way when they were here.'

'Female guests?' Alejandro asked expressionlessly.

'Naturally.'

There was a brief pause. She heard him moving nearer, then felt him sit down next to her.

'Your mother travelled for work?'

She bit back a sad laugh. 'No, she'd go on retreats to "find herself".' She paused. Her mother would routinely just check out of marriage and motherhood. 'After the attic was renovated, I stopped coming down here.' She'd hardly had to come downstairs at all. She could avoid her father's affairs and absence in her own room.

'And what happened to your mother?' That roughness in his voice gave the question an edge.

'Eventually she didn't come back from one of her retreats. Last I heard, she's in Australia. I guess she finally found herself. She gave Dad everything in the divorce—gave up all her material possessions and never came back.' She'd given up her children too.

But Kitty had had the *house* and the things she'd made to decorate it. And she'd had Teddy, when he could bear to be home.

Alejandro didn't say anything in reply to her admission. There wasn't really anything to say and she was glad he didn't bother with platitudes. But of course he wouldn't; he didn't seem to let anything touch him too closely. Or at least that was the appearance he was so determined to convey. But surely there was more than he showed. She saw those quicksilver flashes of emotion. Of depth. How did she push beyond his teasing, suave exterior?

'So your time spent drawing and sculpting led you to study art,' he said, interrupting her thoughts.

'Collection curation in the end.' She hadn't had the true talent to be an artist. 'While you studied…'

'Law, economics, commerce.'

'Oh.' She shivered at the thought of it.

'Very useful degrees.' He nudged her and she heard his short laugh. 'More so than art.'

'It isn't all about making money,' she fired up.

'So speaks someone who has never struggled to make the money to keep a roof over her head, or enough to eat. Would you eat cake when there's no bread left?' he teased.

'I'm not as ignorant or out of touch as all that,' she muttered. 'I just don't see why it all has to be about how much money you can make. I make enough for *me,* whereas you're out to make as much as humanly possible. Self-made guys like you celebrate the downfall of the likes of my father.'

'Not at all.' Alejandro laughed. 'I would never celebrate anyone's failure.'

No, but he was single-minded about success and ruthless in achieving it. He wouldn't give up at a setback; he'd fight back until he'd won in the way he wanted.

'He worked hard, you know,' she tried to explain. 'He just made mistakes. Plenty of them.' She sighed. 'He was trying to groom Teddy to take over the family business but Ted hated it and was hopeless. They fought a lot.'

'And you hung out in the attic.'

Kitty shifted restlessly; somehow she'd ended up talking more about herself and still learned nothing much more about him.

'But you love your father, even though he let you down,' Alejandro said.

'He has his weaknesses,' she replied. 'We all do.'

'I don't.'

She laughed, pleased to hear that amused confidence in him again. 'Yes, you do. You're arrogant and stubborn.'

'What you call weakness, I call strength,' he countered, unabashed as always. 'Stubbornness is determination and it helps me succeed.'

'Bully for you,' she grumbled. 'There's no success that comes with impulsiveness.'

'You think not?' He laughed softly. 'You successfully bring fun. Laughter. The unpredictable.'

'Are you suggesting I'm unpredictable?' she asked archly. 'Coming from you, that's high praise.'

'Are you suggesting that I've finally charmed you?' he teased.

'Oh, no, I still see through you.' Except she couldn't see him at all; she could only hear the warmth in his tone. 'I know you only want one thing.'

Temptation whispered within her. She wanted it too. And she was tired of fighting her attraction to him. Here in the dark, no one would know. Here she could still learn something about him. She could learn the physical. She shivered again. She was too aware of his nearness, of the possibilities.

'It really is pitch-black, isn't it?' she muttered, trying to distract herself.

'Are you scared?' That thread of amusement sounded, warming her.

Honestly, she was always scared when he was around. Not of him but of her reaction to him. She felt him shift beside her. His arm pressed against hers, so did his leg.

'I used to be afraid of the dark,' she confessed distractedly.

'But you got over it?'

'Teddy locked me in here once, not long after we first discovered it. I was terrified. But after a while I got used to it and I refused to let him know how much it bothered me. Then I found it didn't bother me anyway and I didn't have to pretend any more. This became one of my favourite places to hang out.'

'You faked it till you made it?' His chuckle was soft.

'I guess.'

'I like the dark,' he said gently.

'Oh?' She half expected some comment about his liking the dark because he was usually in bed then, but there was a serious note in his voice. 'Why?'

'It's safe—you can't be seen.'

His answer surprised her to silence. What—or who—did he want to hide from? Why didn't he want to be seen? Was he scarred in some way? Her mind raced with questions. She was about to ask but then she heard him—it was almost a whisper.

'You can't be found.'

'You liked to hide?' She never would have guessed that.

He drew in a quick breath. 'Mmm...'

He didn't elaborate. Of course he didn't.

Why had he needed to feel safe?

She reached out, unable to resist any longer—offering the reassurance of touch. His stubble was rough beneath her fingertips. Who was she kidding—this was what *she* wanted. Here, in the dark, no one would know. She couldn't see. He couldn't see. It could be secret, and maybe a little bit magic.

'Catriona?'

'Shh.' She just wanted to explore.

'Do you know what you are doing?'

She smiled in the darkness and leaned closer to press her lips to his jaw. His muscle jerked beneath her lips.

He turned his head towards her and she felt his breath on her face. 'Don't start something that can't be stopped. Not unless you are very, very sure.'

She would never be sure of anything much. Except that right now she liked exploring what she could of him. She liked it here in the dark where she too could hide and neither of them could see. But she could feel.

His hand cupped her chin, he gently traced her lip with the tip of his finger, and she couldn't resist a quick slide of her tongue. His finger paused and she heard his swiftly indrawn breath.

'This isn't a good idea,' he said roughly.

But, before she could reply, he kissed her gently.

'Yes,' she whispered when he drew back.

'Yes, this isn't a good idea or yes this—?'

'Just yes.' She pressed forward blindly, seeking his mouth again.

And it was a good idea. It was a very, very good idea. Her kiss wasn't gentle. She sank into it, relishing the freedom. Here, in the dark, she relinquished her hold on her desire. It burst free—heating the small space. She wanted to explore him. She ached to touch every part of him, to feel the slide of his skin against her own. She wanted—

He groaned and reached out quickly. Unerringly finding her waist, he lifted her onto his knee, capturing her completely.

'I think you like to take risks, Catriona,' he muttered harshly.

'Alejandro…'

He answered her plea wordlessly, his hot mouth crashing down on hers while his hands explored, lifting under her tee. She moaned as he unclasped her bra and her tight breasts sprang free. He palmed them for a moment and she wriggled on his lap, feeling his hard erection digging into her. Oh, yes, this was what she wanted. This was everything she wanted.

She lifted her arms as he tugged the fabric up, ridding her of both the tee and the dangling bra in the one movement. Then he swept his palms over her naked back, pushing her forward so he could kiss her bared skin, working his way across her body until he sucked her painfully tight nipple into his mouth. She cried out as heat flamed low in her belly.

'I want to taste more,' he said gruffly. 'I want everything.'

He moved, lifting her and placing her on her back beside him. It took nothing for him to slip off her shoes and run his hands up her legs to unsnap the fastening of her jeans and then slide them and her panties down and off.

She was naked now. And hot.

'I want to see you,' he groaned.

But he couldn't and she was pleased because here in the darkness she was free. His hands were warm, his mouth hot as he licked his way up the inside of her thigh. Her legs splayed and he took control, pushing them wider to make room for him between them. He kissed her core, holding her in the most carnally explicit position she'd ever been in in her life. She couldn't control the sobs of pleasure as his tongue caressed her, teasing her most sensitive nub with swirls and licks until she shivered uncontrollably. She was so close.

'*Please*,' she begged him. 'I want you.'

He broke free to brace above her, his body pressing against hers in agonising temptation. 'You had to do this now? When we have nothing here? No bed? No protection?' He swore furiously and at length. 'You madden me.'

'We can just…' She drew in a shuddering breath and writhed under him. She was so close. 'I want to touch you.'

He paused and it gave her enough time to reach up, feeling for the buttons of his shirt. She undid them, sliding her hand beneath the cotton to feel the damp, silken heat of his skin. She tracked her hand through the light dusting of coarse hair and briefly wished she could see him. He shrugged off the shirt completely and she lifted higher, so her tongue could follow the path of her fingertips. His skin was warm and a little salty and she wanted to taste more too.

But he slid his hand between them. She moaned as he parted her, exploring. He swore again. She trembled as he stroked her, drawing her tension out, making it impossible to bear. Because it wasn't enough. His fingers, his tongue weren't enough. She wanted *all* of him.

'I can't take it any more,' she muttered brokenly. '*Please.*'

'Please what?'

In the darkness, in the warmth, in the delirium only he seemed to be able to stir, it was safe to speak. Safe to say exactly what she wanted from him.

'Take me,' she whispered in absolute hedonistic abandonment. 'Take me hard.'

'Oh, hell, Catriona!' he ground out, frantically moving against her. 'I can't resist feeling you—I'll ensure—'

She heard the slide of his zip and melted. 'Yes. Oh, yes.'

'I'm clean… I've never had sex without protection in all my life.'

She was so eager she didn't care. 'Just do it,' she begged. 'I want to feel you.' Inside. Here. Now.

'Just for a moment.' He flexed his powerful body, controlled and slow, but she felt his muscles shaking.

'Yes.' Just this once.

She thought she was going to die if she didn't experience it all with him.

He paused. Then thrust. Hard.

'*Alejandro.*'

One word shot from his mouth in reply—crude and very much to the point. But she was too far gone, her body rigid and locked on his. She gasped harshly, clutching him closer, her legs parting that bit wider, wanting him closer, closer still, even as he filled her so completely.

'I cannot stop,' he rasped hoarsely. 'I can't…'

'*Yes*,' she cried, trembling and twisting beneath and about him as her orgasm ravaged her body. So, *so* ecstatic.

Suddenly he moved—hard, rough. Pulling back, only to thrust hard again. His hands tightened, holding her in place so he could drive deeper into her, pumping faster and faster.

'Oh, yes,' she gasped, her breath knocked from her. She rocked, meeting every fierce thrust, pushing their pace faster still, her hands greedy on him. It was carnal and hot and wet, and he was big and bossy and she was going to orgasm all over again. '*Oh, yes.*'

She didn't want him to stop. Not ever. Undone at last, they pounded together, frenetic and free. She was hurtling towards another orgasm, her last barely over. Her mouth parted as cries of delight tore from her. It was so good. *So* good. But at that ultimate moment he suddenly pulled out of her. She arched high but it was too late. He was gone.

His seed spurted over her stomach in hot, pulsing bursts as he braced above her, his agonised groan ripped from deep within.

She moaned too, a sound of torn satisfaction, of frustration. She'd wanted to ride through that tornado of bliss with him this time, but he'd wrenched out of her embrace.

'It wasn't supposed to happen like this.' He groaned again and cursed softly. She felt the absence as he lifted right away from her.

She lay still, shocked by how rapidly their passion had escalated into something so out of control. So reckless. So breathtakingly sensational.

'Like how?' Gingerly, she eased up into a sitting position, licking her dried lips as she felt the literal distance between them growing.

'Over so quick. Too quick.'

And it was over. She didn't trust her voice to answer. Her emotions were all over the place and she didn't want to sound tearful. It had been the most sublime experience of her life but all that exquisite joy she'd felt had been snatched away. Suddenly she felt vulnerable. It had happened. They'd had sex. He'd got what he wanted from her. And now it was over.

'Damn it, what time is it?' he muttered roughly. 'We need to get out of here.'

Kitty didn't want to get out of here. She wanted to curl in a ball and stay hidden for ever. She didn't want to look him in the face again. He'd made her feel things no one else ever had. Never had she enjoyed sex like that before. But it meant so little to him—how could it mean so little?

She realised there was suddenly a small light illuminating his face—in that slight glow he looked serious and distant.

Her body chilled as she realised what he was doing. He was tapping the fancy watch on his wrist. He was sending a damn *message*? Eventually he glanced in her direction and now there was a small smile on his face, as if he was pleased with himself.

Oh, she'd just bet he was.

'Did you just use your smart watch to send an email to get us out of here?' She glared at him even as the light went out and she knew he couldn't get the benefit of the full death stare she had on him. 'Only *now*?'

'Only now, because I just remembered that I had it,' he replied calmly. 'Until now, I was somewhat distracted.'

'But you could have sent a message sooner. Before...' She trailed off then cleared her throat determinedly. 'You could have sent a message when we were first stuck in here. But you didn't.'

'Catriona.'

She didn't answer him. She was too busy whipping herself into a fury.

'Catriona.'

Eventually he sighed and she heard his low laugh but she was not finding anything funny right now. She felt around on the floor for her clothes, not bothering with her bra or undies. She tried wriggling awkwardly into her jeans but they were all twisted and she couldn't figure them out in the stupid dark and she hated knowing that he could hear her struggling and was probably laughing inside at her expense. In the end she shoved on her tee and hoped it was the right way round, and who gave a damn about her shoes anyway.

'Alejandro?' a voice called.

Of course Paolo would arrive in less than ten freaking minutes.

'In here!' Alejandro banged on the door. 'The mechanism is down to your right.'

Alejandro had stood but Kitty remained curled on the floor as far in the corner as she could fit.

Light streamed in.

'Thank you,' he said to Paolo, who'd unlocked the door but hadn't stepped in. 'Please leave us now. Immediately.'

Alejandro moved out of the room, leaving the narrow doorway open. He didn't look back at her, but Kitty could see him—still clad in his suit trousers and shoes. But his shirt was off. He was tall and muscular and just that bare back on show made her shiver. She was glad when he disappeared from view, leaving the entranceway empty. But she heard him talking in a low tone, and his brief, infuriating laugh.

Then nothing.

'He's gone,' Alejandro called eventually when she didn't appear, his amusement still evident in his voice. 'You're safe to come out.'

The *last* thing she was, was safe.

But she stood, clutching the rest of her clothes protectively in front of her as she strode out, determined to pack her bags and leave the house this instant. Damn the diamonds, she'd get the lawyer onto it, as she should have right in the beginning.

She stomped past where Alejandro stood in the hallway, heading straight for the stairs. She didn't even glance at him.

'Catriona.'

She ignored that dangerous edge in Alejandro's voice.

'*Catriona.*'

'I'm not talking to you.' She turned to face him, tried to ignore how devastatingly gorgeous he looked in just those low-slung, unbelted trousers and no damn shirt on. 'You took advantage of that situation. You manipulated it.'

'How did I do that, exactly?' he asked. 'I wasn't the one pleading. Stop acting like a teenager and creating drama where there is none. You wanted me. I wanted you. We still want each other. What does it matter when I sent the stupid message?'

Because she wouldn't have succumbed to him then and there. She could have held out. Because they hadn't needed to sit there in the darkness together and experience that sense of intimacy build. But it hadn't been real. Not to him.

'It doesn't make any difference, Catriona,' he said. 'Our having sex was as inevitable as the sun rising and you know it as well as I.' He ran his hand through his hair, leaving tufts upright and even more gorgeous. 'Don't try to tell me you regret it.'

Only now could she see those muscles and that delicious olive skin of his and appreciate him truly. He was like a god. And only now did she realise what he was holding in his hand.

'You got Paolo to bring you *condoms*?' she shrieked.

'It seemed like a practical solution.' He shrugged. 'I did not have any.'

She glared at him. He probably did that all the time—sent his assistants out for a coffee and cake and another two dozen condoms because he burned through them so quickly. He was a sex-driven devil. But, heaven help her, hadn't she just benefitted from all that wealth of experience?

'Have you *no* shame?' She turned and took to the stairs, furious with him. She heard his laugh behind her.

'You seem to have enough for the both of us.' He grabbed her arm, stopping her, and turned her to look at him. 'Truly, Catriona,' he said softly. 'There are far worse things to be shamed by.'

His words had that core ring of truth to them. But she didn't want to know the truth. She wanted… She didn't know what she wanted any more.

He waited three steps below her, his eyes just that little bit beneath hers. Beautiful, deep brown eyes. That half smile was so sexy. So assured. And so maddening.

Those hot moments in that small dark space had been the most erotic of her life. That was what she rebelled against. That a man she didn't want to like could bring her to her knees like that. So easily. So carelessly. How was she supposed to protect herself from him when he overwhelmed her so completely? How could she not get hurt in this?

'I don't want to want you like this,' she admitted with a raw edge to her voice. 'I'm leaving.'

His eyes narrowed. 'Do you really think you can walk away right now?'

'Why not?' She shrugged, dropping her gaze. 'We've finally had sex. It's over.'

'It is anything but over.'

'Once was enough.'

He laughed outright at that—but now there was little humour in the sound. 'Was it? Then why are you still fighting me? Why all this heated passion if it doesn't matter?'

'What matters is how you manipulated that to get what you wanted.'

'But it was what you wanted too. I'm not the villain here. I did what you asked me to.'

Heaven help her, she hadn't only asked. She'd begged. And she wanted to beg again.

He wasn't going to give her everything she wanted

and needed. But did *that* really matter? She'd thought she'd found that with James and she couldn't have been more wrong. Maybe she did just need a release for once. Something easy and fun and meaningless. Something that wouldn't matter at all in the long run.

'I just hate letting you win,' she confessed.

And she wasn't that much of a prize anyway. Once he'd seen her—once he'd had her again…

'Don't you understand?' He climbed the two steps until he was right in front of her. 'We're both winning.'

'You really want to win this?' She swept off her tee, baring her entire body.

She'd never been as exposed to anyone. Never in the broad daylight like this.

His jaw dropped, his hungry gaze raked down her pale, freckled, angular body. 'Catriona.'

She didn't get the chance to reply or to run. She was in his arms and his kiss was utterly demanding. Utterly dominant.

And she surrendered totally. Her knees buckled and he lowered her exactly where she was, until she was prone on the staircase. He undid his trousers, kicking them off in a fury. That was when she completely forgot about how she looked. All her focus was on him—the expanse of golden skin and the play of powerful muscles just beneath the surface, the masculine whirls of hair on his chest that then arrowed down in a trail of delight to… She swallowed and her womb pulsed at the sight of him. He was physical perfection. She was hurled straight back into that maelstrom of passion and need and unquenched, unbridled lust.

'Please. Please. Please.' Not a plea, a command. She wanted to touch him. Taste. Feel. She was almost in tears with the need to have him.

He left her for a moment, muttering unintelligibly as he struggled to open the box of condoms and sheath himself.

But then he was back just a step below her butt, on his knees between her legs and grasping her hips firmly. He held her high, controlling her position so he could take her as completely, as dominantly as possible. And watch while he was at it—she was sprawled on the staircase before him, so exposed, and he devoured her with raw lust.

For a second he met her gaze; his eyes were dark and intense and so filled with desire. She panted breathlessly, spellbound. Never had she seen passion this raw. Never had she felt it in herself. The strength of it made her shake. Made her hungry. She was more aroused than she'd ever been in her life.

His gaze narrowed. He knew. He saw it in her, felt it in her. His face flushed. She saw his own control slip as his gaze burned down her bared body again—from her jutting breasts to her waist, to her slick, hungry sex.

'I just have to—' He held her firm and bucked his hips, impaling her to the core.

'*Yes.*'

'This time,' he groaned determinedly as he thrust deep inside her again. 'This time we can take our time.'

But there was no taking time for her. Not when he was grinding so hard against her and so deep inside her and all she could see was his powerful body pressing its passionate intent on hers. She was there already. Arched and taut as a bowstring.

'Alejandro!' The orgasm shattered her. She cried in unashamed ecstasy.

'Damn it, Kitty,' he growled as he held her hips more tightly and thrust harder, deeper, his eyes wide and wild as he stared down at her. 'You make me—'

He broke off as a guttural shout burst from him. His veins popped, his skin glistened as he strained, fighting the pleasure that had already consumed him. Because there was no taking time for him either. 'Kitty,' he choked.

She laughed with exultant delight as he thrust that one last time, striving for the ultimate satisfaction with her. She squeezed hard and tight, cresting again as he was ravaged. She rode the rigours rocking his body as his orgasm exploded, and she relished the lack of control he had in that moment.

Serenity and satisfaction flooded her cells as he slumped heavily over her. And then the cold trickle of reality came. She closed her eyes, needing to scrape together some sort of emotional defence. But she was shocked at the uncontrollable, furious chemistry they seemed to share. They'd just acted like wild animals, mating on the staircase in about twenty seconds flat.

Slowly he disengaged and rose to his knees, gazing down at where she still lay, sprawled down the stairs, naked and unable to move. His eyes glinted as he seemed to read her mind. 'You think we're done?' He shook his head as he bent and scooped her into his arms. 'We're very far from done.'

CHAPTER NINE

ALEJANDRO ROLLED ON to his back, appreciating the softness of the mattress beneath him as he pulled Kitty to rest on his shoulder. The bed was better than the hard floor but was too narrow for total comfort. He breathed out, satisfied. Finally he'd managed to have her the way he'd wanted to—taking his time, making her come again and then again before finally letting himself go.

He'd had to make it up to her because in all his life he'd never lost control as quickly as he had when he'd finally first entered her, locked in that little room. Her tight, writhing body had blown his mind, his orgasm impossible to delay. He groaned inwardly at the speed of it. It must have been the lack of condom—the first time in his life he'd taken such a risk. He knew it had been foolishness, but being with her had felt so good, his skin now goosebumped at the recollection. He still didn't know how he'd managed to pull out. It had nearly killed him at the time.

He couldn't take that risk again. He didn't think he'd have the strength to leave her like that a second time anyway.

But he'd had to have her again—especially when

she'd started to build walls between them. That second time on the stairwell hadn't been much better, with his pleasure literally coming too soon. Even with a condom his control had not been brilliant. But *seeing* her body then, watching her response and the emotions flashing in her eyes? She was exquisite—her breasts high, her nipples dusky, her waist narrow and at that private heart of her there was a thatch of that fiery-coloured hair… And it turned out that the skin that had been silken and warm beneath his lips in the dark room was moon-pale and luminous, and gently dusted with rose-gold freckles—they covered her shoulders, arms, breasts, thighs…every part of her. He'd traced patterns of them with his tongue, desperate to taste every inch of her, *fascinated*.

She'd not liked being naked in the light. She'd not wanted to admit how much she'd wanted him again. Her anger had flared. But when it had burned off, pure desire remained. She'd become passion incarnate—as voracious and as victorious as he.

He'd carried her up to the shower, then had her again up here in her bed. Yet, even now, despite the residual ache in his muscles, he felt his hunger stirring.

She was stirring too—wriggling away from him. He turned to read her expression but she was studying the ceiling with grim determination.

'You can leave now,' she said quietly. 'It's a bit cramped in here.'

He froze. Was she ordering him from her bed? Seriously? Before he'd even had the chance to catch his breath and cool down? Not if he had anything to do with it. She was not calling time yet.

'It's not that small.' He inched down determinedly.

'I'm hot.'

His body stiffened in instinctive reaction to the dismissive challenge in her voice. 'Then we'll take off the coverings.' He kicked the blanket to the floor and pushed the sheet to her hips. 'You're sleeping naked anyway.'

And just like that he was ready again.

'I'm not planning on going anywhere,' he muttered, rolling to his side to lean over her. 'Except down on you.'

She was forced to look at him then. Her eyes were wide and dozens of emotions flickered through them. He kissed her before she could argue and worked his way down, down, down...

He woke early in the morning. He blinked at the light streaming in through the windows and saw the clear blue sky. He was cramped and achy all over. In the end he'd slept the night in her stupidly narrow bed. But he'd simply been unable to move—his muscles slammed by total exhaustion.

Now she was snuggled right into his side, her body soft and warm as it encroached on his. Her hair was like a mass of flames across his chest—soft and warming and with a faint fresh scent. He gently lifted a strand to see it glint in the light. His chest tightened and breathing suddenly seemed harder.

He wanted her to wake, yet he also wanted her to rest. He'd woken more than once in the darkness, unused to having someone with him right through the night. But she'd woken too and welcomed him when he'd turned to her, his appetite rapacious again.

Now she opened her eyes with that sense she seemed to have for when he woke. A pair of emeralds glittered at him, filled with accusation. 'You're still here.'

'Yes.' His throat felt raw and his voice sounded gravelly but, given how long and how harshly he'd groaned during the night, he wasn't surprised. 'I'm still here.'

He watched wariness enter her eyes. He tensed in anticipation. Regrets were not allowed. And this wasn't over yet.

She shifted as if to move away from him but he pressed his palm on her back, holding her in place against him. That tight feeling ventured further south—to familiar territory.

'Is that how you greet your fiancé good morning?' He smiled at her and shifted down her body. 'Maybe I should put you in a better mood, hmm?'

To his pleasure, she parted her legs, letting him in. Always he wanted her to let him this close. He adored doing this to her. Teasing her. Arousing her until she thrashed beneath him and begged for it. He didn't think he'd ever tire of hearing her excitement build. Of making her moan for him. Of making her hot and fierce. He smiled as he kissed her slick, sweet core. He didn't take her again, just licked her to orgasm because he imagined she was probably tender today. He'd not been gentle on the stairs. Or when they'd finally made it to the bed. Hell, even he was aching in parts he hadn't realised he could ache in. He blamed that on the cramped little bed.

'Oh… *Yes!*' The cry was wrenched from her as

she clenched her hands on his shoulders, shuddering through another orgasm.

He stifled his groan as his need sharpened. He'd hold back this time. He kissed her gently through the aftershocks, feeling laxness grow within her and seeing sleepiness return to her green eyes. He gently stroked her hair until her eyelids fluttered shut. Then he moved. But at the doorway he turned, unable to resist taking in one long, last look before beginning his day. She was beautiful, enthusiastic and generous, and the most gorgeous challenge. He could hardly wait already.

It was mid-morning before Kitty woke again. She'd slept better than she had in months. She stretched languorously. *Oh, hell.* There were aches in places too private to be named. So many aches. And the worst?

In her heart.

Never could she regret what had happened yesterday. He had won. Totally. But it had to be done with. She'd finish sifting through all the family stuff and get out of here before she got too enmeshed in an affair that was only going to end painfully for her. Alejandro, for all his arrogance and immunity to emotional depth, was too easy to like.

She took her time in the shower, hoping the hot water would soothe her muscles and over-sensitised skin. But she was half aroused again already, just *thinking* of him. It was the most rapacious case of lust ever. Who knew sex could be so addictive, so much fun and so intense? That it could be all those things at once was both mind-blowing and terrifying.

She fought for control over her own damn mind— making herself get dressed and head downstairs and get on with work. Once she was underway with the boxes, she was startled by a repeated knocking on the front door.

'I'm sorry to interrupt you, Miss Parkes-Wilson, but there's a delivery for the top floor.' Paolo didn't look her in the eye as he explained.

She tried to smile but she was mortified. The man had brought condoms when he'd busted them out of that room yesterday! So Kitty looked past him to where a beautifully tailored woman and a couple of brawny delivery men stood in front of a large truck double parked in the street.

'A delivery?' She blinked then stepped aside to let them in. 'Of course.'

Then she saw what it was—a massive, massive bed.

'For the top floor?' she questioned, her voice squeaking. This was going in *her* bedroom?

'Yes, the attic bedroom,' the woman said crisply. 'Mr Martinez requested I dress the bed for him and ensure it's perfect.'

Did he, now? Unable to answer, Kitty stood aside. It was his house now and she had no authority to argue. She went down to the kitchen and hid. A new, massive bed for her bedroom? The guy had serious nerve.

Almost an hour later she heard Paolo calling for her.

'All done?' She stepped out into the hallway, glad when he nodded.

'You don't wish to inspect it?' the woman asked.

'I'm sure it's lovely.' She led them to the front door and opened it. 'Thanks so much.'

She shut the door on them before her blush became

visible to the astronauts on the International Space Station and, with a combination of avid curiosity and outrage, ran back up to her bedroom, freezing on the threshold when she saw it.

He'd replaced her ancient little bed with a monstrosity best suited to a whorehouse, with its four posts perfect for tying dominatrix straps to. Except that was her being overdramatic. It wasn't tacky. It was beautiful. Freshly laundered white linen covered the whole thing so it looked like a soft cloud. The thing that annoyed her the most was that it was *gorgeous* and fitted her room perfectly. And she was turned on just at the sight of it.

She turned on her heel and marched out of the room, determined to get the sorting done even more quickly than she'd planned. The sooner she got away from Alejandro Martinez, the better for her emotional health.

'Darling, I'm back.'

Anticipation rippled through her body. Despite his sarcastic call, she heard the rough edge of desire underneath it.

'What took you so long?' she taunted, knowing full well he was home earlier than usual. Again.

He walked towards her, his gaze penetrating, that cocky smile curving his arrogant mouth. 'I take it the bed arrived? Let's go use it.' He grabbed her hand and led her to the stairs, carrying a plastic bag in the other. 'I walked into the store and chose what I wanted.'

Was this the new routine? *Now* this liaison was exposed as the blistering lust-fest that it was. No dinners out any more—or even in. It was just straight to bed to have sex the second he walked in the door. She ignored her own desire for exactly that—she couldn't let him have it this easily.

'It's too big,' she grumbled as they got to the top floor.

He sent her a sideways look that told her he wasn't fooled. 'I figured we needed a little more space to be creative.'

She was not hot at the thought of that. She wasn't.

In her bedroom he set another box of condoms on the table. She stared at it, feeling the shifts deep within her treacherous body.

'I suppose the best thing is I'll have the space to be able to sleep without having to actually touch you,' she muttered.

'Yes, because you hated using me as your pillow last night.' He stood his ground as he began to unbutton his shirt. 'Why don't you come closer and try to tell me again how much you don't want me?'

She flung her head back, watching as with each flick of his wrist more of his beautiful skin was exposed. 'What's in the bag—sex toys?'

'Dinner.' He laughed and his muscles flexed in the most distracting fashion. 'I'll get the toys tomorrow now I know you want them.'

'Oh, so I actually get dinner?' she asked tartly. 'But it's takeaway. Disposable. Not the five-star restaurants any more.'

His smile was evil. 'I know what you want more.'

Her skin burned as she watched him strip. His muscles rippled; his body was hard and magnetic.

Two could play at that game.

'And I know what you want.' She lifted her top and whisked it off her head. She wore no bra—her nipples were too sensitive for lace today.

He retaliated by toeing off his shoes, then socks and finally kicking off his trousers and boxers in the one movement. Kitty's mouth dried as she drank in the response of his body; her hands shook as she peeled her jeans and panties off. Naked, trembling, she stared at him from across the room in a wordless but passionate duel.

'Come here,' he breathed his command.

Internally she battled—her pride, her need to deny him when he always got it *all*, versus her own desire for him.

No false declarations or meaningless promises.

This was what it was. The dam had burst and there was no containing it now until the lust had been drained. She needed it to be drained.

She stepped towards him until she was close enough for him to grasp her waist and slam her against him in that last step. She arched her neck, granting him full access even as she stared hard into his eyes and challenged him. 'Do you insist on such total surrender from all your women, the way you demand it from me?'

'No.' Despite gritting his teeth, Alejandro couldn't hold back his honest reply. 'There's just something about you that really ticks me off.'

Something that lit him up. Something he couldn't get enough of. Her, like this, naked and hot and welcoming him. Stripped back to the essentials, this was sexual hunger, unstoppable and fantastic. The sooner it was sated the better and it was killing him trying to hold back from thrusting hard and claiming her with no foreplay whatsoever.

He didn't understand *why* she needed to fight him, but he knew she couldn't help it. Something about him got to her. It was the same for him. He relished sparring with her, anticipated her arguments and ached for the moment she surrendered and welcomed him into her hot, wet body.

'So you want me to submit?' she asked.

And she did that now. Stepping back, she fell backwards onto the big bed, her arms and legs spread-eagled, positioning herself like an offering for him, except her eyes were alight with that challenge. She wasn't giving in to him without extracting something in return.

'Is this what you wanted?' she taunted.

He couldn't get the condom on fast enough. 'This is your fantasy and you know it.' He breathed hard, daring her to deny it but needing to hear something else. Something true. 'You like it when I pin you down and kiss every inch of you.'

He'd known from the second he'd seen her that it would be like this—their physical attraction was combustible. He caressed her until he heard her gasp. Slow. So Slow. Until, hot and wet, she sobbed for her release. Never had pleasuring a woman been so pleasurable for him.

'Yes,' she screamed. *'Oh, yes!'*

He rose in a fury, fired by her raw admission.

'You're obsessed,' she murmured as she spread her legs wider so he could take his place where she wanted him.

'Possibly.'

The words were a warning in his ear. Was this un-natural? Was this constant ache going too far? But he couldn't stop now. With a harsh groan, he buried himself deep inside her, growling at the exquisite tor-ment of her tight silken body. He held fast for a mo-ment, just to prove to himself that he could.

'Please,' she whispered beneath him, her arms holding him tight and close. 'Please.'

And there it was. He couldn't resist that request, couldn't deny her or himself. So, in turn, he too sur-rendered, driving hard, driving home.

Strong yet soft, she met him thrust for thrust. *'Ale-jandro.'*

He lay as limp and useless as a rag but despite his exhaustion he couldn't join her in sleep. She was the most sexually compatible lover he'd had. Not that he'd had as many as she seemed to think. It wasn't as if he spent every night with a new woman. Sex was merely a relaxation strategy to combat work hours and stress.

But this was different. This driving resurgence of desire only moments after completion? He felt inhu-manly strong and the voracious hunger drove him on. It couldn't last, right? Usually a few days was enough with one woman before he eased off…but he wanted Kitty more than ever. He wanted so much more.

Any kind of obsession was unhealthy, but at least his obsession with work resulted in a productive, safe, outcome. To be obsessed by a woman? That wasn't safe.

And he was obsessed. He was addicted. Not just to sex with her, but to the way she stood up to him, the way she made him laugh, the way she made him feel alive. And he wondered about the wistful expression on her face as she packed up her family's history from this house, but at the same time he knew the connection she felt to this place was something he could never understand, no matter how hard he tried.

And he did demand her surrender. He was obsessed with that.

God, his brain was addled. Never before had he sat at his desk and discovered he'd lost five minutes in a dream-like state, just thinking about a woman. He didn't want to think about anyone like that. He didn't want to lose control of himself in that way. He'd seen what happened when someone became obsessive. Became possessive.

Someone very much like him.

He couldn't let it happen now. Not with sweet, vulnerable Kitty. Not with anyone.

He had to protect her. He had to remember he had too much to do. Work had to take precedence. He breathed out, finally able to relax and sink towards slumber as he realised: work was the answer.

CHAPTER TEN

'I'M GOING TO New York for a week. You'll be all right here on your own?'

Kitty looked up from her checklist and hoped she'd hidden the way her heart had just thudded to the floor. 'Of course. It'll be a nice holiday from you,' she lied. He was home early again, but he wasn't staying. He was going away for *a week*.

'Me and my lecherous demands?' He caught her close and kissed her until she was soft and leaning against him. 'You're not going to miss me at all?' he teased.

'I'm going to catch up on my sleep.' She pushed out of his arms and brushed her hair back from her face.

It was mean of him to invite an admission like that when he'd never admit such a thing himself. She'd be out of sight and out of mind... She frowned.

'I'll call you and—'

'Don't,' she interrupted breathlessly.

A quizzical expression crossed his face. 'Don't call you?'

'Not if you're going to call me like you did Saskia that night. I'd rather you didn't call me at all. I'd rather not know.'

His eyes widened. 'What are you implying?'

'I just mean that when this is over I want you to tell me face-to-face, not a phone call. You think you can hold back from temptation for a week?' She held her head high, even though she hated how shrill she sounded. 'Because I don't think that's too much to ask of my fake fiancé.' She didn't want humiliation in that way.

'Catriona, I'll be working non-stop—'

'You'll have to eat sometime—'

'So I'll eat at my desk.'

She laughed a little bitterly. 'You won't go out to all those fancy restaurants?'

The ones with all those women who'd love nothing more than his attention and for him to take them home for a couple of hours' post-work 'relaxation'.

'I have a lot of work to do; that's all this trip is. For me to *work* hard. I'll play with you when I get back.'

And that was what this was. *Play.* A game that would be over soon enough. It was good to get the reminder.

She nodded and forced a smile, but it was small. 'Okay.'

She wanted to believe him, but past experience told her she was a fool to. Her father. Her real fiancé. And Alejandro himself wasn't one to maintain a relationship. He'd admitted that he didn't ever want to.

'I'll see you soon,' he said.

'You're leaving now?' She bit her lip as she realised how that sounded.

'Yes. I just called by on my way to the airport.'

For a moment she thought he was going to say something more, but he shook his head.

'Okay, then…' She struggled to think. 'Have a good trip.'

He sent her a sombre look, turned and left.

She stared at the empty space in the room that he'd left. That was it? Had he really gone so quickly—with just a few words?

Better get used to it. This was what would happen when they parted for good.

Swallowing back a horribly desolate feeling, she turned back to her checklist. She *wasn't* going to torture herself imagining him with a million women while he was away. She was going to get the work done so she could get away quickly and cleanly once he did return and keep herself from hurting more. And until then, when he was out of sight, *she'd* keep *him* out of her mind.

But she was lonelier than she'd ever been in her life. The house was too empty, that new bed too huge, the ache in her heart too unrelenting. She needed distraction—and plenty of it.

'What the hell is going on with you two?' Teddy's eyebrows were at his hairline as he poured her a coffee in the theatre's green room. 'You've really fallen for him?'

'It's impossible not to fall for him.' Kitty shrugged and forced a smile as she confessed the truth in the safety of a joke. 'Unfortunately. But he's away and I need something to do.'

Her brother eyed her for a moment, then pushed a mug of coffee towards her. 'We need help,' he said. 'We always need help. No one can source cheap props the way you do. Can't pay, though.'

Kitty laughed, grateful for the support. 'Well, duh.'

She enjoyed the theatre scene. Hunting for props was fun, creating them even more so. While Teddy's play was almost due to open, the play next in the schedule needed some items that she was happy to help conjure up. She hadn't done that in an age—not since before she'd had to get a 'real job' as gallery assistant.

True to her request, Alejandro didn't phone her. But that night he did send her a picture. It was of the empty soup container on his desk. His dinner. She sent him a selfie poking her tongue out at him.

The next night it was a pizza box. The night after that, a noodle box.

Less than halfway through his self-imposed respite week Alejandro wondered, for the millionth time, what Kitty was doing. Where she was. Who she was with.

Unease chilled his gut. Would she be out seeing friends? Would she have finished up at the house and left?

She hadn't wanted him to phone. She hadn't been able to meet his eyes when she'd asked him not to and he'd made her explain why. Now he felt embarrassed about that call he'd placed to Saskia in front of her. What an arrogant thing to do. He arranged for a bunch of flowers and a brief, apologetic notecard to be sent to Saskia. He hadn't meant to be cruel, but maybe he had been. Contrary to what he'd told Kitty at the time, he didn't know for sure if all Saskia had wanted was a quick fling. As usual he'd set out his expectations and just assumed she'd accepted them. But too often people hid their true feelings.

He counted down the days but time crawled. The nights were worse. His sleep was disturbed, but not by desire. Twice he woke with sweat filming his brow. That old helpless despair clogged his throat. He stared into the darkness and thought of her to make himself feel better. And worse. Because he couldn't stop thinking of her.

The fourth night away, he couldn't take it any more. He succumbed to the temptation and called Kitty's mobile. But she didn't pick up. The brief message on her answer service wasn't enough to satisfy his need to hear her voice. He tried the landline at Parkes House. She didn't answer that either.

He paced through his Manhattan apartment, his concentration in smithereens. He needed to know where she was. He needed to know *now*. Was she okay? Had she been in an accident? Was she with someone else?

A billion questions swarmed in his mind, stopping him from thinking properly. Slowly, a cold unease seeped into his belly and began to burn. This obsessing over her was becoming a festering wound. Who was he to demand to know the minutiae of her day? Since when was his head so filled with wonderings about a woman? He did not want to be this man. He'd *never* wanted to be this man—not obsessive, not possessive.

His phone rang and he pounced on it. But it wasn't Kitty; it was one of his junior consultants in the London office.

'I've had a question come up—'

'I'll come back early.' Alejandro fell on the excuse gladly.

'You don't need to—'

'I'll be on the first flight.'

It was night-time when he landed.

'Is Kitty at home?' Alejandro asked Paolo the second he saw him waiting for him at the airport.

Paolo looked evasive as he led the way to the car. 'She said she was happy using public transport.'

Grimly, Alejandro said nothing. Paolo was not a gaoler but he was a protector, and Alejandro should have made it clear that he needed to know she was physically safe and secure at all times.

After Paolo dropped him off, he unlocked the door, his anticipation building. But he knew as soon as he crossed the threshold that she wasn't home. He paced though the house, wondering where she was, who she was with, why she still wasn't answering her damn phone.

Finally, almost two stomach-churning hours later, he heard the key in the door.

She was in her usual black trousers, black top ensemble, not one of the designer dresses. Her hair was tied back and hidden under a black wool beanie of all things. She'd not been out to dinner? She was smiling—looking so happy—and she'd not seen him yet.

'Hey.' He couldn't choke out more of a greeting than that. The wave of emotion at seeing her again was too intense.

'Alejandro.' For a moment she looked shocked. But then her brilliant smile broadened. 'You're back early.'

That reaction soothed him, but not completely.

She put her large bag down and unwound the scarf from her neck. 'Did you miss me too much?' She looked sassy.

'I got the work done sooner than I'd expected.' He couldn't relax enough to walk towards her. 'Where've you been?'

She didn't take her gaze from him. 'At Teddy's play,' she said softly. 'It was opening night tonight.'

'You didn't answer your mobile when I called.'

'Because I turned it off. It's polite to do that when you're at a live theatre performance.' Her gaze intensified. 'Before you ask, I've spent the last few days helping out at the theatre with the props.'

'I wasn't going to ask.'

'No?' She chuckled.

He shifted on his feet, not able to bring himself to walk either to her or away from her. He hated the mess of emotion in his gut.

She came nearer.

'You're not a little jealous?' she teased lightly.

'I don't get jealous.' He couldn't even break a smile.

'No?' Her eyes danced. 'Maybe something you ate disagreed with you.'

'I'm not jealous,' he repeated. He hated this feeling. He wanted it to go away. He wanted her to come closer to him.

'You missed me,' he told her. It wasn't a question.

Her mouth tightened and her chin lifted. 'I missed the *sex*.'

Not a good enough answer. 'Not me?'

'And your grumpy mood? Hell, no.'

He reached out to curl his arm around her waist

and haul her close so she was pressed against him. Hell, *yes*, that was where he needed her. Close.

'Every step of the way you try to deny this attraction,' he said roughly. 'You deny it even as you dance into my bed.'

'There are moments when I don't like you.' Her eyes sparkled. 'But as I'm stuck in this situation I might as well use what little you can offer.'

His body tightened at the insult. 'What "little" can I offer?'

'Orgasms,' she answered airily.

'Is that all?'

She chose not to say anything more. Provoking him.

Alejandro gave her a gentle shake. 'Stop trying to annoy me. You won't like it if I retaliate.'

'You're the one being annoying.' She slipped off her beanie, released her hair from its elastic tie and shook it out. 'You're all talk.'

The anger he'd felt suddenly morphed into something else. The desire to control. To prove a point. Deliberately, slowly he lowered his head. Her response to his kiss was instantaneous and made the passion within him flare. But it didn't soothe the need coursing in his veins. He lifted her and carried her up the stairs, kissing her as he climbed. Passion, anger and relief combined, giving him a burst of strength. He couldn't get her naked quickly enough. But he didn't strip himself. Not entirely. He needed to retain some control for what he intended to do.

He forced himself to slow down, to caress—first with fingertips, then lips, then tongue. His blood quickened as he felt her skin warm, as he heard her breathing change. He knew her well now but it still wasn't enough. He couldn't stop touching her, greedy for the feel of her skin against his again. Need spiked. He wanted to kiss her everywhere, touch her everywhere, take her. *Now.*

Too fast again. He growled, pulling back.

She arched, reaching for him.

'Not yet, Kitty,' he said roughly. 'I don't feel like giving you that yet.'

But he was lying to her and to himself. He held her arms pinned above her head with one hand, and with his other he trailed his fingertips over her skin, feeling that silky smoothness and following the pattern of pretty freckles all the way down. She was so gorgeous, she tormented him. It would take nothing for her to come, and he knew it. But he wasn't giving it to her. Which meant he wasn't coming either.

Stalemate.

Kitty looked into his dark eyes, unable to stop herself arching up to him again. He was here, home, with her, but he was so controlled and so grim and so determined to have her total surrender. But she wanted his too. And she saw the flush in his cheeks, the sheen on his skin. She felt the barely leashed energy in his twitching muscles. The rapacious lust in his gaze only turned her on all the more, but no matter how she provoked him, he always had the last laugh. He always won. Suddenly she was angry—with herself for missing him so much, with him for always teasing and never telling the truth—with him for not acknowledging that this thing between them was…*more.*

Impulse burned. Before she thought better of it,

she lashed out. 'Do you honestly believe I'm thinking about you?'

The look he gave her then was filthy, fiery fury. He
rapidly thrust away from her in a rough motion. She
raised up onto her elbows, watching as he stripped
out of his pants and jerkily sheathed his straining
erection. His lack of finesse proved just how angry
she'd made him. She closed her eyes and slumped
back in heated agony and anticipation. She'd wanted
this. Wanted him to be unleashed. He grabbed her
hips and pulled her down until her lower legs dangled
over the edge of the bed. She felt him step between
her parted knees.

'Open your eyes, Catriona,' he demanded. 'Open
your eyes and look at me.'

He kissed the heart of her and she almost came on
the spot. She cried out when he left her just before
she could crash over the edge.

'Open your eyes.'

This time she obeyed. Her heart thundered as excitement flooded her veins. He was standing over her,
his muscles bunching, his body flushed. She ran her
tongue along her dry lips.

'Say my name,' he said as he spread her thighs that
little bit more with his broad hands and then bent to
brace above her, one fist either side of her head.

'Alejandro,' she whispered, melting in the storm
of arousal and need and anger.

'Louder,' he insisted. 'Don't stop saying it, or I'll
stop. Don't stop looking at me.'

'Egotistical maniac.' She lifted her chin at the
filthy look that flashed in his eyes.

'I just want honesty. Be honest,' he demanded.

He came down hard and thrust into her. One forceful movement.

'Then I expect the same from you!' she cried in his face as the exquisite sensation pushed her past her emotional limits. 'Be honest with me.' She clutched him close, utterly torn between happiness and frustration and the yearning for *more* from him. The need for everything. 'You were *jealous*.'

'I missed this,' he shouted back, his control breaking and he thrust hard and fierce. Uncontrollably, he pumped into her over and over, his passion pushing them both across the bed. 'Missed you,' he corrected brokenly. 'Missed you.' He groaned in tortured surrender. 'God, I missed you.'

'Yes!' she cried, her nails curling into his rigid muscles as she held him tightly.

She'd missed him too. So much. Now she wrapped around him, holding him closer than ever, feeling him there with her. So very *there*. Not just physically but in every way. She gazed into his eyes, swept away on the tide of emotion pouring out of him. Emotion that reflected her own—need, need, *need*.

The orgasm hit too quickly, too intensely. Everything shattered. It was easily the most beautiful experience of her life.

In the end she didn't think she'd ever be able to move again. He was slumped over her, his breathing still ragged, emotion continuing to radiate from him. She stroked his hair back from his forehead. His skin was burning, his face was still flushed from the insane effort he'd unleashed on her. She blinked back the tears that had welled in her eyes then swallowed so she could find her voice.

'I don't know why you make me so mad that I say whatever pops into my head to aggravate you,' she whispered, brushing her fingertips down the side of his face. 'I'm sorry I was such a witch.'

'I was not any better,' he admitted, his voice oddly subdued as he shifted to lie beside her. 'I'm sorry. I was…jealous.'

Peace settled within her as he admitted it and she smiled at him sleepily, her eyes closing.

But he didn't smile back.

Alejandro jolted awake a few hours later. Trying to stay quiet, he mentally counted to regulate his breathing. She was fast asleep, burrowed into his side, and he didn't want her to wake this time, not when his heart was racing, his skin was covered in a cold sweat and nausea roiled in his stomach.

He swallowed hard, his mind whirring as he tried to shut down the nightmare. He breathed slowly, hoping to calm himself. But he couldn't help examining the emotions she'd so easily identified. Emotions he'd never felt before. He'd not let himself feel them before.

He'd turned away from any teen crush, going with the girls who'd wanted something else from him. Something simple. The more he'd had of those, the more there'd been. It had become easy. Just sex. Just pleasure. Nothing deeper.

But now insidious fear crawled just under his skin. Memories scalded, choking him. The malevolence, the neediness, echoed in his head.

'You love him more than me.'

The demands. The obsession.

'You're not leaving. You're never leaving.'

He hadn't had these horror-soaked dreams in years. Hadn't thought about the past in so long. He was fine. Happy. Healthy. Living a great, successful life. But in the last few weeks it had changed. Now it didn't seem as great. Or as successful.

In those days while he'd been in New York, Kitty had been laughing, having fun. She hadn't been missing him at all. Which should be fine. Just as it should be fine for her to spend time with Teddy. How could he be jealous of her *brother*? It wasn't as if he was any kind of threat. Yet here he was, feeling jealous, fighting with her, wanting—what?

His feelings were out of control. *He* was out of control.

His worst nightmare had become reality.

CHAPTER ELEVEN

WHEN ALEJANDRO NEXT woke he discovered Kitty had already left the bed. He glanced at the time. It wasn't that he'd slept in; it was that she'd got up appallingly early.

Why?

He pushed back the sheet and tried to swallow down the burn of regret that she wasn't there for him to touch. It wasn't anywhere near as easy. Hell, he was suddenly so *needy*.

He forced himself to shower and dress before going downstairs in search of her. She wasn't in any of the bedrooms on the second floor, but he noticed how much she'd cleared and sorted. She was almost done. That was good. That had to be good.

He finally found her in the kitchen, working at the covered table with a soldering iron in hand, bent over an incredibly weird-looking object. 'What are you doing?'

She glanced up, guilt flashing on her face even as she smiled. 'I hope I didn't wake you.' She looked back at the mass of plastic, metal and wire she was working on. 'I know I should be finishing those last few boxes, but I promised Teddy I'd get this done in time for their rehearsal later.'

He stepped closer to the table. 'What is it?'

'A prototype gamma-ray shield for an intergalactic army.' A self-conscious giggle escaped as she set the soldering iron down. 'The next show at the theatre is a cowboy space opera.'

'Of course it is.' He leaned down to take a better look. 'You made it from scratch?'

She nodded and he was aware of the anxious look in her eyes.

He took a moment to study it. Yet to be painted, she'd constructed it using who knew what and had included details that most likely wouldn't be seen from the stage. It was a miniature work of art. 'It's amazing. Can I pick it up?' When she nodded he lifted it. 'It's so detailed. And exactly what a shield should be like.'

She flushed at his tiny compliment, which both pleased and annoyed him. Why hadn't her family complimented her more?

'But not too heavy?' she checked.

'No.' He carefully tested the weight. 'It's good.'

'Hopefully, if they like it they'll offer me more work. Paid, even.' An excited smile lit up her face. 'I can do it when I've finished here.'

When she left him? He stared, hating the feeling washing through him.

Her cheeks coloured slightly and she looked back to the shield as he carefully put it back down.

'You should come and see Teddy's play.' Her words were rushed. 'He's actually pretty good.'

'You're very loyal to him.' To the point of doing some breaking and entering even.

'Of course. He's my twin—I have to be his number

one fan.' She rolled her eyes as she laughed. 'Don't you have any brothers or sisters?'

'No.'

He'd answered too tersely. Now he sensed her biting back follow-up questions. Of course she was curious; he would be too. He walked away so he couldn't see her expressive eyes. He might as well get it over with; she'd have to find out eventually. Obviously she hadn't done the stalker-style Internet search on him that he'd done on her. He shouldn't feel put out by that. He shouldn't feel half of what he was feeling. The nightmares had left a residue of discomfort which left him tired and irritable. Telling her would be good. It would be the beginning of the end.

'My mother is dead,' he said bluntly. 'My father killed her in a jealous rage because she dared try to leave him. The police shot him.'

His blood rushed to his head, making the room spin, and he put his hand out to the wall. He'd not had to say it aloud for a while. He'd forgotten how much it impacted. He tried to count in his head. That numbness that he'd employed for so long came in handy now.

'What?' Her voice was a shocked whisper. 'Alejandro...'

'Everyone knows,' he said brusquely. 'There's no point trying to hide it. It happened. I was a child. I have accepted it and moved on.' He licked his very dry lips. 'I was sent to the States to live. I was very lucky.'

He had been very lucky. After the first two shots, his father had pointed the gun at him. He'd been seconds away from death when the police had killed his father. His mother had been lying just in front of him; she'd stepped forward when she'd seen what his father had in his hand. Nothing could take that image away from him. Nothing could lessen the impact. Nothing could change it.

And he could never be the man his father had been.

'Where were you?' she asked.

'That's why they shot him. He was pointing the gun at me.'

Alejandro turned to look at Kitty in time to see two fat tears rolling down her cheeks. Her simple, heart-rent reaction touched him more than words ever could.

'I'm okay,' he muttered quickly, his breath shortening. 'Better than okay. I was fostered. I focused on school. It was my way out. I got good scholarships. I studied really, really hard.'

Somehow he was standing right in front of her and his arms were around her. She leaned in.

'You're not supposed to comfort me—it's supposed to be the other way round.' Kitty wrapped her arms around him, holding him as tight as she could, wishing she could absorb even some of the pain that was intrinsically bound within him.

He'd told her that truth so baldly, so mechanically.

She wanted to ask so much more. Wanted to know when, how old he'd been, who'd helped him... But it all seemed so inane, those details unnecessary, because they couldn't change the pure horror of what he'd endured. It couldn't make it better. Nothing could make this any better. What about the poor child who'd witnessed that brutality? Who'd lost his mother at the hands of his father?

No wonder he lived his life determined to skate along the superficiality of good times and simple fun. He didn't want complicated. He didn't want emotional.

He didn't want to be hurt again.

'So that's why you don't want marriage or children,' she said when she lifted her face.

'Why would I?' he answered bluntly.

Why, indeed.

'Don't try to change me,' he said softly, his voice a little rough.

'I wouldn't presume to think I could,' she whispered.

'Don't pity me.'

'Don't try to dictate how I'm supposed to feel.' How could she not feel sorry for him, knowing this?

'You only need to feel pleasure.'

His hedonism made total sense now. *He* only wanted pleasure. Only light and easy fun. But life was never like that. Not in the end.

He'd built an impenetrable shell around himself. Always out, always with people, always having fun. Always that superficial delight. No real emotional intimacy.

'I only want fun,' he warned her one last time.

She gazed at him, then slowly nodded. 'Then let's have fun.'

Alejandro jolted awake. Again he froze so he didn't disturb her, but his heart raced as he blocked the lingering image in his mind. He tried to focus on work instead. But that didn't help much either. Alejandro stifled a groan of despair. He had to go back to New

York tomorrow but he was dreading it. He already knew time and distance from her weren't going to help him regain his perspective. He'd thought that if he indulged in her for a couple of days, he'd have had enough. Instead he just wanted more. He liked the way she teased him. He liked listening to her talking about the house, the theatre, the restaurants. He liked her. Maybe telling her about his past had been a mistake—it had broken a barrier within him and she seemed to be able to slip closer than before.

Now he was worried.

He didn't want to feel the gaping loss he'd felt the last time he'd left her—not that massive 'something's missing' sensation. He didn't want that worry, nor the nagging jealousy of nothing. If she was with him, he wouldn't feel that.

Too tired to resist the temptation, he turned and gently roused her. It only took a moment. 'Come with me.'

A twinkle lit her slumberous eyes. 'I did already.'

'No. To New York. Come with me.'

She froze mid-stretch, suddenly looking unsure. He hated that wariness in her, as if she couldn't trust or believe what he was saying.

'I don't want to have another night without you,' he said, her vulnerability forcing him into honesty. Then he smiled. 'Come wear your ridiculous dresses over there. I dare you.'

He made himself work for a while on the plane— just to prove he could. But the rest of the time he sat comfortably as Kitty curled next to him, engrossed in the movie she'd selected. The limo ride to his apartment took too long and it was dark when he finally led her into his building. It wasn't until he'd flicked the lights on and turned to see her reaction that he realised her pallor.

'Are you okay?' He stepped forward and grabbed her shoulders. She looked as if she was about to fall down at any second.

'I'm just really tired.' She grinned apologetically. 'Like really, really tired. I think the flight got to me more than I thought it would.'

'Then straight to bed.' He led her to the guest bedroom and put her bag just inside the door. 'Come on.'

'I want to explore first.' But she stepped into the room. 'Wow, fancy.'

He glanced around at the sleek interior, with its private bathroom with his-and-hers basins. This wasn't his room; this was the room he used when *entertaining*.

He frowned as he followed her back into the living area. 'You like it?'

'It's very tasteful. Very different to Parkes House.'

'Less full of stuff, you mean.'

'Yeah.' She winked at him and made a beeline for the bookshelf.

But it wasn't the books she was checking out. It was the photo.

'My mother,' he explained, even though he knew it was obvious.

'She looks like you.' She smiled at him shyly. 'Except for your eyes.'

An acrid feeling burned in his throat. 'I have my father's eyes.'

She glanced at the shelf but of course there was

no photo there of his father. No other photos at all. For the first time he thought about how boring his apartment must look. The only personal things in it were his books.

'I think you're right,' she said quietly. 'I really need to get some sleep.'

He looked at her; she'd paled again. And suddenly he didn't want her in that bedroom. He didn't want the memory of other women in there with them. He wanted it to be theirs alone.

'Come with me.' He led her up the spiral staircase to his secret space and opened the door to let her past him. 'This is where I usually sleep.'

Her eyes widened as she looked at the small room, her mind processing. 'When you're alone.'

'Yes.' It was small and very simply decorated, safe and quiet, up high on the mezzanine floor. 'You'll sleep better in here.' He cleared his throat. 'It's darker—the curtains are...' He was making excuses. He just didn't want her in that other room.

'Okay,' she said. 'Thanks. I'm sorry I'm so tired.'

So was he, but not because he was desperate to slake his lust. He wanted her to be okay. 'Don't worry, just sleep.'

He climbed in beside her and drew her close so her head rested on his chest. Slowly he relaxed as he felt her sink into sleep in his arms. Warm weariness stole into his bones, and that feeling of anxiety eased until he slept too.

'Alejandro?'

His eyes snapped open; his heart was thundering. Kitty was leaning over him, her eyes wide and worried. He realised the reading light beside her was on and—

'Are you okay?' He sat up and checked his watch. It was only just after two in the morning. 'What's wrong?'

'N-nothing.' She eased back, turning away from studying him so intently. 'I'm fine. I just…'

He waited, rubbing his hand through his hair. His forehead felt damp—had he been dreaming again? He froze.

'I just—I don't know about you, but I'm *starving*.' Kitty suddenly slid out of the bed and sent him a dazzling smile. 'I'm going to go fix something.'

Food? Fantastic. 'I'm not eating noodles,' he muttered.

'Who said I was cooking anything for you?' she said tartly, her spirit snapping. 'Honestly, your arrogance…'

He laughed and rolled out of the bed, inordinately happy that she was back to her best. 'I'll cook. But I can't believe I have to cook vegetarian.'

'You've never used any of this, have you?' She looked around the sterile kitchen while he headed to the pantry, praying he had something edible in there.

He stepped out, brandishing a couple of cans and a bag of rice. The freezer revealed more possibilities.

'Are you sure it'll even work?' she teased as he flicked a switch on the oven. 'I bet you've never turned it on even once before.'

He grinned at her. 'You know I'm very good at turning things on.'

She rolled her eyes.

'Not noodles,' he said pointedly as he placed a

steaming dish of rice and vegetables in front of her fifteen minutes later.

'Oh, so good,' she mumbled after the first forkful. Then she glared at him. 'Is there anything you aren't good at?'

'So many things,' he said lightly. 'I won't bore you with the list.'

Only a few hours later, when he got up to go to work, he tried not to disturb her, but she sat up anyway. She still had shadows beneath her eyes. He frowned. He'd been selfish, all these nights of interrupted sleep had taken a toll on her. He'd been little better than an animal. But she'd wanted it too. She'd pushed him. She'd welcomed him. Even so, she clearly needed a break.

'Lie back down and sleep in,' he told her.

'And miss the chance to explore New York?' she pretty much shrieked. 'Never.'

'Please.' He wanted that pallor to return to a more normal shade. 'Just have a couple more hours' rest then meet me for lunch. I'll send a car.'

'I can find my own way.'

That determined independence annoyed him. It was so unnecessary. But he knew there was no point arguing.

In the end she stood him up for lunch. She sent a text saying she'd meet him back at the apartment before dinner. Apparently she'd got distracted at the shops.

Disappointed, he worked through, but he was glad she must be feeling better. They'd go out tonight, just the two of them. He contacted a friend to find out the city's best vegetarian restaurant and then phoned to secure a table, bribing his way in.

When he finally got home she was ready.

'Where are we going?' she asked before he'd even said hello.

For a moment he didn't answer; he was too busy staring. Now he understood why she'd got distracted. She was in a designer dress, but it wasn't black. It was a beautiful bottle-green and cut to perfectly emphasise her slim waist. The low-scooped neckline showed her delectable freckles. The first time she'd ever worn anything that revealed them. The first time she was in colour. She looked stunning.

He saw the wary hesitancy in her eyes and the way she was holding herself very erect, and knew he was going to need to tread carefully. If he said the wrong thing she'd flare up at him. And for once he didn't want to do that. Maybe there wasn't a right thing to say. Only a right thing to do. He walked to her and cupped her face in his hands.

'Look at me,' he commanded softly when she avoided his eyes.

Slowly, reluctantly, she met his gaze.

'I can't kiss you or we'll never get out of here tonight,' he muttered hoarsely. 'You've gone to too much trouble to stay home.' For once it hadn't been for anyone else. It had been for him. It touched him more than he could bear. 'You are beautiful.'

She pushed back from him, not meeting his eyes as she blushed. 'You'll sleep with anything.'

'You really know how to insult a man.' He grabbed her hand so she couldn't walk far. 'But you insult yourself the most.'

He had no way to prove how attractive he found

her. No way other than sleeping with her—again and again and again.

'I'm not a beast who roots whenever, however, with whatever I can,' he said bluntly. 'I can sleep with none but the world's most beautiful women. A list of models a mile long. Yet I choose to screw you. And only you. Over and over. Why do you think that is?'

'You're going through a phase.'

He laughed and released her hand, giving up on convincing her. 'You wish to burn yourself with insecurity about your appearance, that's your choice.'

Her head whipped as she turned to stare at him, her jaw slack. Suddenly she laughed.

'What?' He queried the change in her demeanour. All of a sudden she was *glowing*.

'You're right.' She giggled again and actually wiped a tear from her eye. 'You're absolutely right. I've been stupid.'

He cupped her face again. 'Not stupid.' He knew she'd not got the security she needed from her father or her ex-fiancé. 'Sweet.'

She tilted her chin, her eyes glinted, her lips still curved. 'Not that sweet...' she murmured wickedly.

'No,' he muttered hoarsely. 'We need to leave. We're going to the most lauded vegetarian restaurant in the city. You've no idea the hoops I had to jump through to get us a table at such late notice.'

Delight shimmered and she leaned even closer. 'You're going vegetarian for me?'

'Just for tonight,' he drawled. 'So for once you get to choose anything from the menu—you're not limited to one or two same-old, same-old dishes. So let's go.'

But she didn't move; she just smiled up at him and his chest was too tight again and he couldn't seem to move. His heart couldn't pound hard enough. She was sparkling now—her eyes glittering like jewels.

'Kitty—' He pulled the diamond choker from his pocket.

Her soft lips parted as she gazed at them, then back up at him. 'You have it with you?'

'All the time.' He didn't know why. He felt close to her when he had it in his breast pocket. It was stupid, but there it was. 'Please wear it.'

It would look stunning on her.

She shook her head, her smile resolute. 'I can't. It's not mine to wear.'

'You wish it was?' He'd buy them for her if he could.

'It's just not meant to be that way.' She turned away from him.

She deserved more than that. She ought to have her heart's desire. She had such a generous heart.

'You took such a risk for them.' He smiled as he remembered her stealing in to the library that night, all sleek determination and fire.

'Isn't there someone for whom you'd do anything?' she asked lightly. 'No matter the cost or the risk?'

He maintained his smile, but an emptiness gaped in his stomach. She loved in a way he couldn't. The cost of loving like that was too great.

CHAPTER TWELVE

'KITTY?'

It couldn't possibly be morning. It just couldn't. Kitty groaned as she opened her eyes.

Alejandro was already up, dressed in jeans and looking gorgeous as he held a mug towards her. How had she slept through his getting up? She always woke when he did—and not just in the morning, but in the middle of the night when he had those dreams that made his whole body flinch and her heart ache because she didn't know how to help him. The dreams that seemed to be occurring more and more frequently and were more and more frightening for him.

'Coffee?'

'Oh, no, thanks.' She tried to turn her grimace into a smile and rolled over so he couldn't see how bad her attempt was. But the smell was making her gag. She screwed her eyes tight shut and wished she was back in that warm, deep sleep. Yesterday, as the day had worn on she'd felt better, but once again she'd woken feeling so very tired. And queasy as—

Her eyes flashed open and she stared at the white wall of his cosy private bedroom. *Queasy?*

Her mouth filled with bitter spit and she forced

herself to swallow it back without moving. Her feminine intuition had kicked in way too late. When was her cycle due? She frowned. She was usually pretty regular and she should have had her period at the end of that first week that Alejandro had been in New York. But she hadn't had it and she'd been so distracted she'd not stopped to think about it at all. Until now.

'I thought I'd take the day off,' Alejandro said huskily as he sat on the edge of the bed. 'Thought I'd come with you on your sightseeing trip today.'

Her heart would have leapt if it wasn't too busy beating at a billion thuds per second.

'Oh.' *No.*

Not today. Not this. Oh, please, not this.

She shrank into the mattress as her mind scurried. She needed time to figure herself out. Time to reassure herself that she was panicking over nothing and only having an irregular few weeks or something. Her pulse hammered in her ears as she tried to think of an excuse to put him off. 'I'm still feeling tired—I think I need to sleep some more. Maybe later today?'

But he'd offered to take time from work and spend it with her—and she had to turn him down…? She bit her lip, holding the heartbreak and fear inside.

'Are you okay?' He leaned over her and looked at her intently. 'Do you need to see a doctor?'

'No,' she lied and avoided his eyes. 'I'm just tired.' She forced a coy smile. 'I guess I'm not used to the all-night bedroom antics the way you are.'

She felt him withdraw at that flippant comment, but she hardened her heart. She had to have a couple of hours to herself this morning because she was too anxious to maintain a facade of carelessness until later.

'Text me later then.' Alejandro stood. 'I'll see where I'm at.'

'Okay.' She forced herself to snuggle back down in the bed.

He paused on his way out of the room, then turned and walked back to where she was, now almost totally hidden in a tight huddle under the sheets. 'Rest well.'

He pressed his lips to hers. At first she was too scared to be able to relax into the kiss but then that warmth flooded her, overwhelming her as it always did. As *he* always did.

But the moment she heard the door close she sprang out of bed, ignoring the return of the bitter taste in her mouth.

She quickly dressed and then took the elevator down to the ground floor. She smiled confidently at the doorman as he held the door for her to leave the building. She wasn't going to make the mistake of asking him for help finding a pharmacy—that information would be bound to filter back to Alejandro at some point.

She strode along the busy pavement, trying to look as if she knew where she was going. Down two blocks she finally stopped and asked a café worker for assistance.

Five minutes later she handed over the cash for the home pregnancy test. Her fingers were freezing and she almost dropped the change. The chances were so very low, right?

But their first time in that secret room... Surely there'd be only the slightest risk from that? He'd pulled out before he'd orgasmed. How unlucky could they be if a baby had been conceived in that so-brief moment?

Back in his apartment the result flashed almost immediately.

Pregnant.

Kitty stared fixedly at the result, her brain working overtime. She repeated the test. And got the same result.

All kinds of emotions swooped in so quickly she felt faint. She sat down on the floor of the gleaming bathroom. This could *not* be happening.

But it was. Slowly, a feeling of utter certainty and conviction stole over her, giving her an unexpected sense of calm.

She ran her hand over her still-flat belly. There was a tiny life in there. Alejandro's child. Her heart almost burst beneath a wave of unconditional, absolute love. Her muscles flexed in a surge of protectiveness. And suddenly she didn't feel unlucky at all.

But then she thought of Alejandro and how he would react to this. Her ballooning heart ruptured and she gasped as she realised the hurt they both faced.

This was the very last thing he wanted and it was the very last thing she wanted to do to him.

He didn't want this. He didn't really want her—not for good. Her eyes filled as she realised the happiness she'd felt in the last few days had just been a facade.

She quickly stood. She had no time for tears. She had to leave. She had to think about how she was going to handle everything before telling him. She had to have a sure plan in place before she could even *face* him.

Galvanised into action, she methodically packed her clothing and left the building again with another confident wave at the doorman. She rounded the corner of the block before hailing a cab and heading to the airport. She used the last of the available credit on her card to buy a ticket for the next flight back to London.

She switched her phone off and left it off—from the time she left his apartment, through all the hours during the flight and the time she travelled across London. When she switched it on to phone Teddy, it rang immediately.

Alejandro.

Her heart spasmed. But she didn't answer it yet. She couldn't. Not until she'd figured out a plan that would work. He didn't want marriage, he didn't want children and she knew he wasn't going to change that stance—not for her. But she had that tiny fear that he would try to 'do the right thing'—that he would be as chivalrous and generous as she knew him to be.

So she had to show him that she could handle all of this on her own. That it would make no difference to his life. That he could remain free.

The fact was, he would have lost interest in *her* soon enough anyway. She'd been that temporary aberration, a different kind of fling for him. But her heart sputtered in a last little fight at that thought— she'd started to believe it might be something a little more special than that.

But that wishful thought could never be tested now because she would *never* use this pregnancy to lay *any* kind of claim on him. She had to shut him out for now, until she'd proven her total independence.

'Kitty?' Teddy sounded puffed as he answered her call on only the second ring.

'Yeah—'

'Alejandro has been calling me round the clock wanting to know if I knew where you were and if you're okay. Are you okay?'

She closed her eyes. 'I need your help. Please. Where are you right now?'

Teddy spoke rapidly, his concern audible, but she couldn't tell him anything yet either—only that she needed a safe haven, and quickly. She didn't stop at Parkes House—she went straight to Teddy. And, from him, to a train.

It was another ninety minutes after seeing Teddy before she summoned the strength and courage necessary to phone Alejandro himself. By now she'd been operating on automatic flight mode for so long, it wasn't difficult to sound detached. And that was good. She just had to keep blocking the pain for a few moments longer.

'Where the hell are you?' Alejandro demanded as soon as he heard her voice. 'Kitty, what's happened?'

'Nothing. I just realised I'd made a mistake and wanted to return to London.'

'A mistake?' he queried harshly.

'It's over, Alejandro.' She couldn't get her voice above a whisper.

'What kind of mistake?'

'Coming to New York with you. Us having an affair.'

There was a pause.

'Is there someone else?' he asked, a different tone in his voice. Fear.

Kitty shut her eyes tightly and grasped hold of the excuse he'd just handed her. 'Yes.'

'I don't believe you,' he said bluntly. 'Something's happened. Tell me what's happened.'

She swallowed and repeated her stance, determined to stick to her game plan for forcing him away from her. 'It's very simple. I've met someone else. I wanted to tell you before you found out some other way. It was fun while it lasted.'

Alejandro stopped pacing across the floor of his empty apartment and listened harder, trying to ascertain something—anything—in the resulting silence.

'Kitty?' He couldn't believe she'd just said that.

Now he replayed the cruel words in his head and realised that they echoed those he'd said to Saskia those few short weeks ago. Saskia and every other woman before her. The irony wasn't lost on him. And now his anger began to build.

Had she done all of this deliberately? Was she out to teach him that 'lesson' she'd long ago said he deserved?

'You're back in London?' Now he'd heard from her and could tell that—physically at least—she was safe, he was sure of it. 'I'm on the next flight.'

He walked out of his apartment and locked it as he spoke. He'd been packed and ready for the last twelve hours while he'd been desperately trying to track her down.

'Don't!' she suddenly snapped, her voice rising in pitch and volume. 'You won't find me, Alejandro. Accept it's over and move on.'

She ended the call.

For a moment sheer rage blinded him. He'd find her and find out the goddamn truth or—

What? What would he do?

His blood iced but bile boiled up his throat. Shame burned at how angry he'd felt less than a second ago. And, now, how hurt he felt.

But as he replayed her last desperate words in his mind, he heard the pain evident in her tone. Something was wrong. Very wrong. And when Kitty was hurt or upset she ran away. She'd run to Cornwall when her fiancé had cheated on her. She'd gone to her secret room as a child when her father had let her down.

It was what she always did.

When he called her phone back again she didn't answer. Not the first time. Or the fifteenth.

CHAPTER THIRTEEN

TEDDY PARKES-WILSON STRAIGHTENED up and shook his head. 'I'm never going to tell you where she is,' he said before Alejandro had a chance to speak. 'Say what you like. Do what you like. You'll never get it out of me.'

'Relax. I'm not about to beat it out of you.' Alejandro stared into the younger man's eyes. 'I wouldn't ask you to betray her trust. I wouldn't expect you to and I wouldn't respect you if you did.'

He shoved his hands into his pockets, hiding the way his fingers had curled into fists in frustration. But he meant what he'd said; he wasn't about to bully anyone. That was the whole point. 'I know you're loyal to her,' he said to Teddy, unable to hide his bitter censure. 'Even though you take advantage of her.'

Teddy looked annoyed, but accepting. 'That's why I won't tell you. I owe her and I know it.'

Alejandro had known Teddy wouldn't give his twin up. But he wasn't giving up either. 'I will find her.'

'Even though she doesn't want you to? You'll still hunt her down?'

'Yes.' Alejandro forced himself not to flinch, hating the way Teddy seemed to think he was some kind of monster—what had Kitty said to him? 'Because she and I need to resolve this face-to-face.'

He needed to see her one last time. If only to understand. If only to reassure her that she didn't need to run away from *him*. He didn't understand why she'd run and the least she could give him was that explanation. He refused to be someone who was feared. That was his worst nightmare.

'I think this belongs to you.' He pulled the diamond choker from his pocket and held it out.

Teddy's face flooded with colour in that sudden way his sister's did. 'It does, but I don't deserve it.' He took the necklace. 'I'll give it to her.'

Alejandro walked out of the small rehearsal studio none the wiser as to where Kitty actually was. Not Cornwall this time—that would be too obvious. Not Corsica to be with her father. He guessed she'd probably used some of Teddy's resources. But he had resources too. And he'd use every last one of them to track her down.

He hated the darkness of his thoughts, yet he couldn't stop them consuming his mind and time. He couldn't bear the thought of her with another man and refused to believe she actually was. Yet doubts wormed. Jealousy festered. He had to know the truth behind why she'd ended it.

He had to know she was okay.

But it was almost a full month since she'd left New York before his phone buzzed with a profitable call from the private investigator he'd engaged weeks earlier. A month in which Alejandro had worked around the clock. A month in which he'd been unable to sleep, in which he'd not gone out to dinner because he couldn't face the feeling of isolation in crowded places, in which he'd paced the empty rooms of her former family home and wished she was there with him.

A month of hell.

'There's a crofter's cottage on the Highland estate of one of the brother's theatre friends that's sometimes rented out as a holiday home,' the investigator said briskly but with obvious excitement in his tone. 'It's been booked out for the next few months.'

'And she's there?'

'I believe it's her but I'm sending you a picture now for confirmation.'

Alejandro rang off and stared at his phone impatiently, waiting for the photo to land. When it did he drew in a sharp breath and was glad he was sitting down. His muscles emptied of energy. His heart stopped.

The shot was taken from a distance but with a long lens to get a close-up on her face, which meant it was slightly blurry. But he instantly recognised her. She was wearing a woollen coat—black, of course—and her hair was loose. Her skin was as pale as ever, her freckles as pretty. But there were no sparks in those emerald eyes.

He phoned the investigator back. 'Give me the address.'

'I've texted it to you already.'

Alejandro closed his eyes. 'Is she staying there alone?'

'Yes.'

He cut the call, groaning in bitter relief. He'd go

there this instant. He broke into a run, storming out of his office in the early morning, abandoning the meetings scheduled and not giving a damn.

He worked out it was fastest to fly to Glasgow and drive from there. But it still took too long—hours of adrenalin, of a mounting headache that threatened his vision, of a tightening in his chest that made it hard to breathe. Hours of trying to work out what to say to her first.

But when he finally parked up outside the small cottage in the early evening he could see at once that it was empty. The curtains weren't drawn, there were no lights on, no other vehicle on the driveway. He clenched the steering wheel of the plush rental car and bit back his bellow of frustration. Had she somehow heard he was on his way? That was impossible. He'd told no one where he was going.

He got out of the car anyway to peer into the windows of the cottage and see if any of her stuff was visible. In the first window he couldn't see much. There was an open-plan lounge and kitchen with a number of impressive paintings on the wall, a plump armchair placed near the window to catch the sun and the low table next to it had a used teacup and a book on it, but there were no identifiable clothes draped anywhere…

He realised the barking in the distance was growing louder. He stepped back from the window to walk along the small veranda and rounded the corner so he could see behind the cottage.

An Irish red setter bounded towards him ahead of a slim figure walking behind it. She wore a beanie but her fiery hair flowed out from underneath it. And she wore black, of course. Not the cute little tailored trousers; this was an exercise combination—leggings and a sleek merino top that clung to her...*curves*.

She'd been out for a walk. There was colour in her cheeks. That colour drained the second she saw him.

Alejandro's eyes narrowed as he stared hard back at her.

For a heartbeat her pace faltered. Her hand lifted in a barrier across her belly. A small giveaway gesture of protectiveness. That book on the table inside flashed in Alejandro's mind. The title that he'd seen but not really registered.

Pregnancy & Beyond: A Guide to Baby's First Year.

And the expression in Kitty's eyes now?

Guilt.

'How did you find me?' Her voice shook as she neared enough for him to hear her.

He couldn't answer. He couldn't stop staring at the changes in her body—tiny changes, yes, but even in the slimming black attire they were obvious to him. Her breasts were fuller, as was her slender belly. She was pregnant. He was certain of it. And he knew to his bones that it was his.

This was why she'd left him.

He only needed to look into her eyes for a second to know what she was going to do and he'd not expect anything less from her.

She would have the child. She would love the child.

For a second he was blinded and his gut burned. Molten rage scoured his ribs. He had not felt so hurt since—

He shut his eyes. Blocking the memory and the wave of emotion that threatened to overwhelm him.

This was not what he wanted. This was *never* what he'd wanted.

'*That bastard's blood—*' he choked. Unable to move. Unable to utter another word.

He'd never wanted this. Never, ever. He'd wanted the whole sorry mess to die when he did. He'd forced himself to forget it for almost all of his life. It was over. Only now it wasn't.

'Alejandro—'

He threw out his hand to stop her from stepping nearer to him. He was too angry.

'I need time,' he snapped. 'You've had…*weeks* to get used to this. Give me…give me…'

Kitty stopped in her tracks as shame burned. He *knew*. He'd found her and he knew and he was so very angry.

She didn't blame him. She should have told him so much sooner. But the days had slipped by and she'd been focused on finding a quiet place to settle for a while. On keeping well. On *hiding*. She'd been such a coward. But she couldn't be now. She swallowed and made herself speak.

'I'll be in the cottage,' she said quietly. 'Whenever you want to talk.'

She wouldn't blame him if he got back into his car and drove away. He'd hate her for this and maybe he was right to. And wasn't that what she'd wanted? Hadn't she done this deliberately to force this kind of response from him?

Yes, she was that much of a coward.

But she left the door to the small cottage open and stood with her back to the door because she couldn't cope with watching him, waiting to see what he would

choose to do. The dog let her know when Alejandro
stepped inside. She turned as he barked and saw him
run up to Alejandro, his tail wagging crazily as he
nuzzled Alejandro's hand, asking for a pat.

Alejandro complied, but he didn't look down at the
animal. He was too busy staring at her and so obviously keeping himself in check. Emotion burned in
his eyes. The trouble was she didn't know what emotion it was.

'Are you keeping well?' he finally asked.

'I'm fine, Alejandro. I'm okay.' She walked over
to him and closed the door.

He didn't take a seat, though; he just stood there—
too large for this room. Too big for her heart.

She saw his pallor and the torment in his eyes and
her willpower broke. She couldn't help reaching out
to cup his jaw. But he flinched and pulled back before she made contact. She curled her fingers into a
fist, hurt by his rejection even when she knew she
deserved his anger.

She turned away. 'I'll put the kettle on,' she said
lamely.

'Don't,' he said shortly. 'This won't take long.'

She hadn't got even halfway across the room. Now
she turned back to face him.

'So there is no one else?' he said quietly.

She lifted her chin. 'There's the baby.'

The emotion in his eyes flared as she referred to
it. Confirmed it.

'I know you don't want children,' she said quickly.
'That's why I left. I don't expect anything from you.
I never will.'

He turned on his heel, strode to the window and

stared out of it at the darkening sky. 'You didn't give me a chance. You ran away without talking to me. You have made your decision without me,' he muttered in a low voice. 'I suppose there is nothing more to be said.'

Yes, that was what she'd wanted, right? For him to say nothing. For him not to fight. Not to try to 'step up' and be the husband and father to her child that secretly she so very badly desired. But having him behave as she'd thought she wanted him to hurt.

'You might not want this child, but I do,' she said defensively.

He turned his head and glared at her. 'You want it for the wrong reasons.'

What wrong reasons? 'To trap you into paying money to me?' she guessed wildly. Her hurt morphed into sudden, vicious anger. 'I said I don't want anything from you.'

Which was a lie, but what she truly wanted she could never have.

'You want this baby because you want someone to love you,' he snapped.

Shocked, she just stared open-mouthed at him, feeling as if she'd been ditched—hanging fifty feet up a cliff with no foothold. 'I wasn't the one who didn't bother with the condom. I wasn't the one who—'

'All your life you've wanted someone to adore you and now you think you've got it,' he interrupted coldly.

'I didn't *plan* this—' she fought back.

'But what are you going to do when it gets hard? Are you going to run away and abandon it when times are tough?'

'Of course not.' She flung her head, stung by his attack. 'And you know what? There's nothing wrong with wanting to be loved.' She burned inside—so wounded, so bereft. 'Or with wanting *to* love someone. At least I'm not afraid to put myself out there and *try*.'

His nostrils flared as he whirled to face her, his stance widening as he braced.

But she stepped forward, too hurt to stop.

'You don't let anyone into your life. Not properly. You basically buy their company with your success and your…skills.' She saw him flinch but she carried on anyway. 'It's not the sex that bothers me. It's the *superficiality*. You keep everything shallow so you can't be hurt.'

He paled in front of her and she felt a twinge of remorse. 'I cannot imagine the horror you experienced as a child… But you're stopping yourself feeling anything except shallow pleasure. You use sex as a temporary muscle relaxant. You're worth more than that.'

And so was she.

'You don't understand,' he said gruffly.

'Then help me understand. Talk to me.'

'The way you talked to me?' He stared at her pointedly.

She slumped into a seat. 'I'm sorry, okay? I'm sorry I didn't tell you.' She glanced up at him. 'I'm sorry if I hurt you.'

'It's not about stopping me from getting hurt,' he muttered. 'When I came back from New York that first time I was away from you, I was jealous of your *brother*.' He closed his eyes for a moment and then looked at her bleakly. 'I can't become that obsessed, Catriona. I can't become that monster.'

She straightened, surprised at his bitter words. 'You'd never be a monster.'

He threw her a pitying look and shook his head at her naivety. 'It's started already,' he argued. 'I took you to New York because I couldn't bear the thought of wondering what you were doing. Who you were with. What I was missing out on. Am I going to become so controlling that I can't leave you alone? That's not normal.'

In that moment hope sparked within her. Had he felt that deeply about her? Did he want more than just a temporary fling with her?

He looked tortured. 'I never wanted to spread the poison that's in my veins.'

Now she realised the hell he was putting himself through. She put her hand across her belly. 'This is a totally innocent baby. Just as you were a totally innocent child. You're not him, Alejandro—you'll *never* be him.'

'I have his eyes.'

'You have your own eyes. You're your own person.' She'd had no idea that this was what he feared. Was this what caused his nightmares?

But he shook his head. 'I can't take the risk. I can't get…' he glanced down at her body and then back up to her face '…I can't get involved.'

It hurt to hear him say it so bluntly.

'Are we not worth the attempt?'

He didn't even want to *try*. She understood that he was hurt, but it hurt her too. So much. Why couldn't someone ever love her the way she loved them? What was it that was wrong with her? Why did she have to miss out again?

'You deserve better than this, Kitty. Better than me.'

That wasn't true—she deserved better *from* him.

'Everybody struggles with their emotions sometimes.' She attempted a smile as she tried to reason with him. And to be as honest as she could. 'I've been so jealous of all those women of yours. I've been so insecure.' She still was. 'But I keep on *trying*. You're worth it to me. This is worth it.'

'So worth it, you ran away without giving me any kind of explanation.' His cheeks looked hollow; he was even paler than before.

'I was scared.'

'Of me,' he said heavily.

'Not because I thought you'd hurt me physically. It was just that I wanted more than you wanted to give me.' She drew in her lip and bit down on it hard. But there was no reason to hold back now. 'I want you to love me. Because I love you.'

He shook his head. 'That can't happen.'

'Because you don't want to get hurt again?'

'Because I cannot do to my child what my father did to me,' he corrected her furiously. 'He ripped me apart, Kitty. He destroyed everything I had.'

'Not everything. You're still here. You've rebuilt so much. People get help for all kinds of issues…' She stood up and walked towards him. 'Why let him steal your future? Your happiness?' She reached him, her heart thundering. 'By shutting yourself away you're letting him win.' She gazed into his beautiful troubled eyes. 'He didn't want anyone else to have your mother. No one else to have you. You're letting him win by locking your heart away. You should show him the middle finger and fight to have a full and happy life. You could get some help; I could help—'

'I can't be the man you need me to be,' he snapped. 'I can't be him. I just can't.'

The finality in his tone devastated her. 'Because you don't love me.'

Not enough to want to try. That was what hurt so much. Not her. Not even the tiny baby she carried. Always, she wasn't enough.

'It's because I *do* love you that I can't,' he roared.

'What?' She stared at him fixedly. 'What did you say?'

He looked back at her; that emotion in his deep eyes was nothing but heartbreak. 'Don't,' he whispered. 'Don't, Kitty.'

Don't make him say it again? Don't make it harder? Don't step closer?

Her eyes filled with tears as her heart broke for both of them. Why couldn't he try for her? She framed his face in her hands, feeling the roughness of his evening stubble. His skin was so warm and he was so beautiful to her. Her heart filled to bursting—with disappointment, with desire, with aching love. She reached onto her tiptoes and kissed him.

He was as still as a statue as she kissed him. But he wasn't cold like marble—he was hot and straining as he held back. She didn't want him to hold back any more—not in any of his emotions.

She kissed him more deeply—winding her arms around his neck. She didn't care about anything else in this instant. There was no point in trying to argue any more. In trying to think. In this one moment of life there was only the need to touch and to feel him again. To have him with her.

To love him.

His hands came to her waist and she pressed closer to him, needing to feel his strength against her now more than ever. And she wanted to reassure him somehow. She wanted him to know how she felt. She wanted him to believe that this could work. This strong, gentle man was so scarred that he couldn't see himself as he really was.

He kissed her back now and suddenly turned her so her back was pressed to the wall—his natural inclination to dominate resurging. She welcomed it—helped him, shimmying down her pants as she leaned back against the wall and then fought with the zip of his trousers. She needed him in this way at least. She'd missed this so much—the searing, unstoppable attraction. The need to take and be taken. She sealed his mouth in that hot, deep kiss, silencing any opposition of his or the spilling of more of her secrets. The kiss told him everything anyway.

She wanted him. She needed him. She loved him.

For once it wasn't the culmination of a challenge, or the finale to a playful flirt. This was nothing but pure emotion. A final kiss, a final connection. All the pain of goodbye. All the love that was being lost.

'Please.' She arched in readiness as he angled her hips in that delightfully sure way. He was hard and she was wet and he pushed to his hilt in one powerful thrust. She cried out at the physical pleasure—at the emotional pain. She felt such completion and yet her heart was being torn apart.

'I'm so sorry.' His voice broke as he paused, looking into her eyes with such torment in his. 'I never wanted to hurt you.'

'It doesn't matter,' she muttered as he gave her the one thing he could.

It was worth it. It would always be worth it.

She rocked her hips, riding him, their coupling hot and wet and as easy as always. But tears coursed down her cheeks as she met him thrust for thrust. He brushed them away but they kept tumbling.

'Kitty,' he pleaded as he pressed deeply into her again and again. His brow was wet, his frown pained. 'I'm sorry.'

Fearlessly, unashamedly she looked into his eyes—she would not hide her feelings from him now. She wrapped her arms more tightly around him and kissed him again and again and again. She loved him. She loved doing this with him. She would never regret any of it. And she never wanted it to end.

But all of the emotions were too big for her to hold—they had to burst free from her. She cried out as the sensations became too exquisite for her body to bear.

He buried his face in her neck. He shuddered violently and his pained, pleasure-soaked groan rang in her ears. She squeezed hard—holding him as deep and as close and for as long as she possibly could. Because it was her last moment with him.

But in the end the intense spasms of pleasure wreaked havoc on her muscles—rendering her limp and weak and leaving her with nothing but words.

He was still. Silent. And, in some ways, stronger than her.

In another heartbeat it would end.

'I love you, Alejandro,' she whispered. 'And I would have loved you no matter what.'

He didn't reply—no word, no look, no action. For one last breath she had him with her. But then she felt his muscles ripple. He flexed and then disengaged—from her body, from her embrace. It took only a moment for him to straighten his clothing and step back from her. His head was bowed so he avoided her eyes. But she wasn't afraid to look at him. There was nothing to be afraid of now. The worst had happened. *Was* happening.

She watched as, without a word, he walked out of her life.

CHAPTER FOURTEEN

KITTY RECEIVED A parcel from Alejandro's lawyer less than a week later. Delivered by courier, the documents explained that a large settlement of money for the child was to be held in trust, together with a monthly allowance that was enough to house, feed and clothe ten children, not just one tiny baby. And he'd gifted her Parkes House and all its contents. No strings. No reversion to the child once he or she was of age. It was hers and hers alone.

There was a note in the letter, penned by the lawyer, informing her that Alejandro was returning to New York and that he planned to stay in a hotel on the occasions he needed to return to London for his work.

She knew he'd avoid it as much as he could. He'd almost never be there.

Her heart solidified. He might be trying to mean well, but she didn't want any of what he was offering her. Not money or physical security.

Time stagnated. The days dragged, but the nights were the worst—she paced, unable to sleep. She missed him. Ached for him. Loved him. And was so angry with him.

A few days later she heard the sound of a car pulling up outside the cottage. Her heart raced for the first time. She opened the door. *Alejandro?*

'Hey, sis! You went quiet—' Teddy broke off from his cheery greeting as he got out of the car and stared at her. His expression morphed to total concern. 'Kit—'

'Don't,' she begged him. 'I know I look... Don't say anything.'

'Jeez, you better get back inside and sit down.' He followed her into the cottage and sat on the sofa opposite her armchair. 'Talk to me.'

'I'm okay, Teddy.'

'Oh, sure you are.' Her twin rolled his eyes. 'You've seen him then?'

She nodded. 'It's finished.'

Teddy frowned then reached into his pocket. 'Alejandro gave it to me.' He handed her Margot's diamond choker. 'But let's face it. It ought to have been yours in the first place.'

Kitty curled her fist around the gleaming coils of platinum and diamonds so she couldn't see it. 'Would you be devastated if I sold it?'

'Why do you want to do that?' Teddy looked shocked.

'Because I need to be independent from him. I can get some capital from this, then sort myself out.' If she was having this baby on her own, she didn't want anyone else to have to pay for it.

'Are you sure the two of you can't work it out?' Teddy leaned forward. 'He looked a wreck. So do you.'

Kitty closed her eyes. 'It's more complicated than... It's just better this way.'

'But you're both miserable. I don't see how that's better than trying to sort it.'

'He doesn't want to try, Teddy,' she said brokenly and the tears finally tumbled. 'That's the point. He doesn't want to *try*.'

Half an hour later, Kitty's tears were dried and she was curled up in the chair watching her brother as he made her a couple of pieces of toast that she didn't feel like eating but knew she had to.

Alejandro wasn't coming back; she accepted that now. No more waiting for a car to arrive. It was over between them. He'd made his decision and she had to move on too.

Maybe Alejandro had been right. Maybe she did run away when times got tough—but not any more.

And maybe part of her wanted this child because she wanted someone to love her. Was that so terrible? But she was the parent here and she was damn determined to ensure that her child felt utterly, *unconditionally* loved. No matter what. Her baby would never feel like he or she wasn't good enough, would never come second to another all the time. Kitty would do everything she could to make her child emotionally whole and secure and happy. The hurts of past generations would not be passed on by her.

And it was beyond time that she pulled herself together and got on with it.

'Can I get a lift back to London with you?' she asked Teddy as he handed her the plate of hot buttered toast.

'Of course.'

New York. The city in which to forget everything. The city where he could get anything, everything and anyone.

Except the one he wanted.

Alejandro stood up from his desk and shrugged on his jacket, ready to go to one of his favourite restaurants. Now was the time to get on with his life. He'd been in a kind of stasis during that month when he'd been unable to find her—he hadn't been able to go back to 'normal' until he'd cleared the air with her. But now he'd done that. More than that, he'd made provision for her and the baby.

His conscience was clear. He'd done all he could.

He'd enjoy his life again. He just needed to get on with it again.

'We haven't seen you here in a while, Alejandro.' The maître d' smiled at him. 'Your guests are already at your usual table.'

'Thank you.'

He'd return to his easy, shallow social whirl.

But it wasn't easy. They welcomed him with bright smiles and barely veiled curiosity that he ignored. He listened to the dinner party chatter. It now seemed inane. Where was the passion? Where was the love for something—anything—other than a party? He glanced around the table, unable to raise a smile. The women were intelligent and beautiful, the men equally talented and all were competitive and driven.

'Are you ready to order, sir?' The waiter interrupted his thoughts.

Alejandro put the menu card down. 'Actually, I've changed my mind. I'm sorry everyone—' he cast a smile around the table '—I won't be dining with you tonight after all.'

He decided to bury himself in work instead. That

at least he was passionate about. That at least was productive.

He worked such long hours he lost track of when it was day and when it was night. That was the good thing about having offices in different countries—one was always open. There were always emails to send and markets to watch. Nightmares to avoid. Loneliness to deny.

Who are you going to leave your billions to?

He thought about a tiny baby with hair the colour of a bonfire. Once he'd let that thought whisper in, the rest tumbled behind it in a flood. The memories he'd been blocking for days. The way she'd challenged him. The way she'd laughed with him. The way she'd looked at him. The way she'd held him.

I love you, Alejandro.

She'd felt so good. But then she'd looked so sad. And she was right—he was such a coward. She deserved so much better than him.

So become the man she needs you to be.

He fought against that little voice—the nagging thread of hope. Of possibility. The dream. He was doing the right thing already. She'd get over it. She was better off without him and the risk he bore.

It was almost midnight several days later when the email landed. He stiffened when he saw Teddy Parkes-Wilson's name as the sender. Had something happened? Was she well? Surely Teddy would phone if it was something bad?

He clicked to open it, suddenly fearful of what her brother was emailing about. He'd pulled the investigator off her. Her life was hers; he was not spying on her. He was not becoming that creep.

But there was no message in Teddy's email—only a link to another website. Great, he was being spammed by her brother. He clicked the link anyway.

It took him to an online auction site—specifically to a series of listings from one vendor. His eyes narrowed as he recognised the first few items. All those designer black dresses. Those shoes. Kitty had placed everything she'd bought with his money up for auction. There was a highlighted comment in the blurb on each stating that all the proceeds would be donated to a leading charity for the survivors of domestic violence.

His throat burned. Shame hollowed him out. But he couldn't stop scrolling down. There were so many memories attached to those dresses. Even the ones she'd not had the chance to wear.

He paused when he came to the emerald dress that she'd worn that last night they'd had together in Manhattan. But it was the entry just beneath that which broke his heart.

The antique diamond choker. This time the proceeds were not listed as going to charity. Alejandro knew exactly why.

Teddy had given it to her and she was using it to gain a foothold on her future. He knew the money in the account he'd set up for her had been untouched. She'd save it for the child but not use a cent for herself. Her integrity and pride wouldn't let her. Now she was doing what she thought she had to do, to make her way independently. She was willing to sacrifice something she loved, for the benefit of some-one else. She always put others first, even when it wasn't necessary.

Well, not this time. He wasn't letting her.

CHAPTER FIFTEEN

'WHAT DO YOU MEAN, the auction site is down?' Kitty glared at the wall as she tried to understand what the man on the helpline was telling her. 'None of my items are up there any more.'

'I know; we're looking into it. We can phone you back once we've located the issue.'

She didn't want them to phone her back; she just wanted it fixed. But she hung up with a sigh and turned back to her new creation on the dining table. She needed to keep focused, keep working, keep moving forward.

Someone banged on the front door just as she was about to begin sketching a 'laser nozzle' for the interstellar transporter. She wiped her hands and went to the door.

'Alejandro.' She stepped back almost instantly, suddenly self-conscious in her splattered tee and ancient leggings. He might have helped her address her body confidence issues, but she'd still rather not be in her painting rags.

'May I come in?' he asked.

He looked better than the last time she'd seen him—not as pale or angular. His eyes were brighter and vitality radiated from him. That was good, right? He was obviously doing well.

But it ripped her heart all over again.

'Of course.' She brushed her hair behind her ear. 'It's still your house.'

He didn't respond to that as he walked in ahead of her. Nervously, she ran her hands down the sides of her legs and followed him.

'You're making more props?' He turned into the kitchen and noted the clay sticking to her tee with a small grin.

'Yes.' She summoned a smile to match his. 'They liked the shield and commissioned more.'

'I'm not surprised.'

She nodded and then looked at him, her heart thudding. 'How can I help?'

He drew his hand from his pocket. She gasped as she saw what he held—Margot's diamonds.

'Where did you get that?' she asked.

'You're not to sell it, Kitty—it means too much to you.'

'How did you get it?' She'd left it in the safe at the auction house.

'I bought it.' A wry grin crossed his face. 'It and several rather stylish dresses.'

'You *didn't*. From my auction?'

He nodded.

'You bought everything?' That was crazy.

'I know it's stupid, but I couldn't bear to think of anyone else wearing them.'

'But you paid for them all *twice*.'

'I don't care.'

'Oh, Alejandro.' Tears pricked her eyes. He melted her, every time. 'Why did you do that?'

Alejandro turned and walked away from her. There was too much he had to say and he lost track of everything when he looked at her. 'I need to tell you about my father.'

He heard her sharp inhalation.

'You don't have to do that.'

'I do. Please.' He took a seat at the furthest end of the table from her so he wasn't tempted to touch her. He had to get this off his chest. He had to get her to understand. 'I don't like to talk about it much, but there's a lot I remember. There'd been other incidents before that day. He was possessive. Jealous. He hit her. And me.' He dragged in another shuddering breath. Saying this aloud to her was harder than he'd thought it would be. But he'd worked on it with his new counsellor, and he was determined he'd get himself sorted. For himself and for Kitty. 'He'd get jealous of me. He'd say she spent more time with me than with him. That she loved me more than him. Like it was a competition.'

Kitty didn't say anything; she just came forward and sat in the chair next to his.

His father had been wrong. His father had been evil. But he had his blood in his veins.

'When she took me and left him for good, he flipped out.' Alejandro avoided looking at Kitty's face as he said it. 'He tracked us down and came after her. She stepped in front of me. She died protecting me.' It hurt so much but he could never forget. And until now he'd never really understood what had driven her. 'That's what mothers do, isn't it? They fight for their young. They'll do anything for their children. Fathers should too.' He lifted his head and looked at her. 'And fathers should love their daughters every bit as much as they love their sons.'

Her sweet face crumpled. 'Alejandro—'

'I think my father confused love with possession. He held on to her and refused to let her go because he saw her as *his*.' He fought back the emotion clogging his throat. 'And I promised myself I was never going to be like that with any woman. I wasn't going to marry. I wasn't going to have kids. It was all so clear and so easy for so long. And then you stole into my new home and I turned into a demanding creep.'

'No—'

'I locked you in the library,' he growled. 'For heaven's sake, Kitty, I was awful to you that night.'

But she shook her head. 'You weren't that bad. I was the one who'd broken in. I was the one in the wrong.'

'But I took advantage of that. I saw you and I wanted you so I used every chance that came my way to keep you with me.' He'd taken total advantage of everything to do with her. 'All you wanted was what should always have been yours. The necklace.'

'But I also wanted you,' she said softly with a small shrug. 'I took one look at you and…you fascinated me. Maddened me. But I wanted you the second I saw you. You were more honest about that than me.' She licked her lips. 'And then I got to know you. You didn't bully me into staying there with you. You didn't threaten me with violence. Not once.'

'But you had to stay only because I had something you wanted.'

'What I really wanted was you.' She smiled sadly at him. 'And if I had really wanted to leave, you wouldn't have stopped me. We both know that.'

Did they? Would he have let her walk out? Not with the diamonds, but without. Yes, he would have.

Her smile deepened as she watched him. 'You would have figured out the ownership of the necklace and returned it. You're not dishonest. You're just. And that night with the necklace was the catalyst for the attraction between us. My staying here was convenient for us both. It's just that I couldn't admit it at the time. I never wanted to admit how attracted I was to you because it overwhelmed me. But I stayed and then really got to know you. That's when I was really in trouble.'

Alejandro couldn't dare believe that she truly cared for him. He didn't deserve it when he'd been so arrogant and so damn dismissive. 'I don't want to make you unhappy. I don't want you to feel trapped. I need to be able to let you go. I have to let you go.' He ruffled his hair distractedly, unable to get the words right. 'Because I'm afraid of myself.' He looked up at her. 'But now I'm more afraid of life without you. I'm so sorry I walked away from you that day in Scotland, Kitty. I'm so sorry.'

Kitty was struggling to believe that he was here. That he'd bought all those dresses all over again. That he was gifting her the diamonds.

Most of all that he'd opened up to her about his father and about his fears.

And she was too afraid to really question why. She couldn't bear to have her heart broken twice over.

'There's something I need to tell you,' she said quickly. 'I had my first pregnancy scan yesterday.'

He paled and she saw the fear flare in his eyes.

'It's okay,' she added quickly. 'Everything is okay.' She swallowed. 'Better than okay in some ways.' She breathed out, struggling to stay in control. 'I'm having twins.'

'Twins,' he echoed softly, his eyebrows lifting.

'Two babies. Twins. Yes.' She still couldn't believe it herself. 'That's why I'm showing so much more at this stage.'

'I thought that was just because you're not very...' He trailed off. 'Twins...' He looked dumbfounded.

'Yes. It's in the family.' She half smiled.

But his expression was shuttered.

She kicked herself for the reminder about genetics and the passing on of particular traits. 'Not that we inherit...'

'No, it's okay.' He huffed out a breath. 'It's just that I don't want you to think I'm here because of the baby... Babies.' He rubbed his hand through his hair. 'The pregnancy isn't relevant—it's you I want.'

Her pulse pounded loudly in her ears and she was glad because she was terrified of hearing what he was going to say next.

'Kitty—'

'You know that marriages with multiples are more likely to fail?' she interrupted in a rush. 'Financial pressures. Lack of sleep. Extra stress.'

He smiled at her—a slow, tender, vulnerable smile. 'We won't have financial pressures and we can get help—nannies, cooks, cleaners, whatever it takes. We're in a better position than most. The thing is,

I don't know how to be a father,' he said huskily. 'I didn't have a good example.'

She shifted on her seat, moving nearer so she could hear every one of his almost whispered words.

'And I've never had a relationship last much longer than a month.' He leaned closer to her too. 'But I want it all with you, Kitty. I want you. I love you.'

'I don't really know how to be a mother yet, either,' she offered shyly. 'A bit of instinct maybe, some help from the experts, and we'll be okay.'

'More than okay. I know I need help processing everything.' He looked intense. 'I know you know about the nightmares. I hadn't had them in so long, but then with you I guess everything opened up...' He trailed off and cleared his throat. 'I thought I had it all together, but I didn't. I wince at the way I treated those women. I was cavalier. I thought I was doing no harm. But I was.'

She reached out and framed his face with her hands. He needed to stop beating himself up. He needed to believe in himself the way she did. 'You're okay, Alejandro. You're a good guy. And I love you.'

'You've changed my life,' he said simply. 'I love you so much. I want to be the man you need. I'm going to be.'

There was the determination she loved in him.

'You already are,' she promised him. 'You *are*.'

A half smile lit in his eyes and he reached into his pocket. 'I got this for you.'

There was a rushing in her ears as he opened the small box and she saw the diamond ring.

'The jeweller worked round the clock to match

the style to the choker, but if you don't like it we can get another.'

'I don't want another.'

'You don't have to wear it.'

She laughed through her tears. 'Stop it. I love it. You didn't have to do that—just coming here was enough. All I wanted was *you*.'

'Oh?' He reached into his pocket again, some of his cocky arrogance returning. 'But I got these too. For, I don't know...next week?'

She stared at the heavy matching wedding bands in his palm.

'Too soon?' There was an edge of anxiety in him now.

'No,' she whispered. 'Oh, Alejandro.' She launched into his arms. 'I need to feel you again,' she confessed. 'So much.'

His laugh was brief but exultant and he stood and quickly turned, flinging the rings to the floor so both his hands were free—to hold her close. Caress her. Claim her.

The kisses were fiery and frantic and the fabric separating their bodies tore. But then, just when he was so nearly hers, he stilled.

'I've missed you.' He trembled as he held back. 'I don't want to hurt you—'

'You won't. It's okay. I want you so much.'

He was gentle anyway, holding her protectively in his arms as they reconnected again in this most intimate, most emotional of ways.

'I love you,' he told her.

Again. Then again. Until her tears flowed and he kissed them away and made her sigh in unbearable pleasure. She'd never imagined it was possible to be *this* happy.

'Two babies,' he breathed hoarsely as he rolled onto his back and lifted her so her head rested on his chest. 'Heaven help me if they have red hair.'

'And freckles.' She mock-shivered. 'The poor kids.'

'They'll be lucky to have them,' he said, idly tracing hers now with a lazy fingertip. 'They're beautiful on you.'

She pushed up and rolled so she was astride him. She shook her head, letting her hair tumble to tickle him, and delighted in the way he looked at her. Finally, she believed in them both. 'You're crazy.'

He smiled into her eyes, relaxed and free, able to enjoy the tease. 'About you. Absolutely.' He kissed her tenderly. 'Always.'

* * * * *

If you enjoyed
CLAIMING HIS CONVENIENT FIANCÉE,
why not explore these other
Natalie Anderson stories?

THE FORGOTTEN GALLO BRIDE
THE MISTRESS THAT TAMED DE SANTIS
THE SECRET THAT SHOCKED DE SANTIS

Available now!

#3549 CARRYING THE SPANIARD'S CHILD
Secret Heirs of Billionaires
by Jennie Lucas

After one night with ruthless Santiago Velazquez, Belle Langtry finds herself carrying a miraculous baby! Belle's news shocks Santiago—he won't let her escape his claim to her *and* their child! His plan? To bind Belle with his ring!

#3550 THE SECRET HE MUST CLAIM
The Saunderson Legacy
by Chantelle Shaw

Elin Saunderson's night with mysterious Cortez left her pregnant! A year later she learns that he will inherit her adopted father's fortune. Cortez Ramos sees one tempting solution: a marriage of convenience, legitimizing his heir *and* returning Elin to his bed!

#3551 A RING FOR THE GREEK'S BABY
One Night With Consequences
by Melanie Milburne

Loukas Kyprianos's wild night with innocent Emily Seymour was unforgettable. But then he finds out that Emily is carrying his child! Emily doesn't expect a fairy tale—but when the Greek's protection turns to seduction, how long will it be before she succumbs?

#3552 BOUGHT FOR THE BILLIONAIRE'S REVENGE
by Clare Connelly

Being forced to spurn Nikos Kyriazis devastated Marnie Kenington. Years later, he offers to absolve her family's bankruptcy—*if* she marries him! Nikos wants revenge—and he knows that in the bedroom he can take Marnie apart, piece by sensual piece...

*Being forced to spurn Nikos Kyriazis devastated
Marnie Kenington. Years later, he offers to absolve her
family's bankruptcy—if she marries him! Nikos wants
revenge—and he knows that in the bedroom he can take
Marnie apart piece by sensual piece...*

Read on for a sneak preview of debut author
Clare Connelly's *book*
BOUGHT FOR THE BILLIONAIRE'S REVENGE.

"Now you will marry me, and he will have to spend the rest
of his life knowing it was me—the man he wouldn't have in
his house—who was his salvation."

The sheer fury of his words whipped Marnie like a rope.
"Nikos," she said, surprised at how calm she could sound in
the middle of his stormy declaration. "He should never have
made you feel like that."

"Your father could have called me every name under the
sun for all I cared, *agape*. It was you I expected more of."

She swallowed. Expectations were not new to Marnie.
Her parents'. Her sister's. Her own.

"And now you will marry me."

Anticipation formed a cliff's edge and she was tumbling
over it, free-falling from a great height. She shook her head,
but they both knew it was denial for the sake of it.

"No more waiting," he intoned darkly, crushing his
mouth to hers in a kiss that stole her breath and colored her
soul.

His tongue clashed with hers. It was a kiss of slavish possession, a kiss designed to challenge and disarm. He blew away every defense she had, reminding her that his body had always been able to manipulate hers. A single look had always been enough to make her break out in a cold sweat of need.

"No more waiting."

"You can't still want me," she said into his mouth, wrapping her hands around his back. "You've hardly lived the life of a monk. I would have thought I'd lost all appeal by now."

"Call it unfinished business," he responded, breaking the kiss to scrape his lips down her neck, nipping at her shoulder.

She pushed her hips forward, instinctively wanting more. Wanting everything.

Her brain was wrapped in cotton wool, foggy and filled with questions softened by confusion. "It was six years ago."

"Yes. And still you're the only woman I have ever believed myself in love with. The only woman I have ever wanted a future with. Once upon a time for love."

"And now?"

"For…less noble reasons."

Don't miss
BOUGHT FOR THE BILLIONAIRE'S REVENGE,
available August 2017 wherever
Harlequin Presents® books and ebooks are sold.

www.Harlequin.com

9118

⬦ HARLEQUIN™ *Presents*®

New York Times bestselling author Maisey Yates draws you into tales of enticing passion with her Once Upon a Seduction… series! Next month, look out for *The Prince's Stolen Virgin*—and read about an innocent, awakened to forbidden temptation by a prince's kiss…

Ordinary Briar Harcourt is horrified to discover her life is a lie—she is, in fact, a long-lost princess, sent into hiding to escape a forced marriage to a brutal king. But now his son, Prince Felipe, has found Briar, and he is determined to claim her as his bride!

Marriage to Briar will give Felipe the power he was born for: her compliance is nonnegotiable. But his searing, uncontrollable desire for her is unexpected…and he'll use all his formidable charisma to seduce her into surrender!

The Prince's Stolen Virgin

Available August 2017

Also from the Once Upon a Seduction… series

The Prince's Captive Virgin

Available now!

The Italian's Pregnant Prisoner

Available October 2017

HP06086